MW01243786

Correspondence to the author can be found at:

www.heavenswars.com

www.facebook.com/heavenswars.com

The sale of this book without a front cover may be unauthorized. If the book is coverless, it may be reported as "unsold and destroyed" to the publisher, and neither the author nor the publisher has received any payment for this "stripped book."

This book is a work of fiction. Names, characters, places, events, incidents, dialogue, and plot are the products of the author's imagination or are used fictiously. Any resemblance to actual persons, living or dead, or to actual events is purely coincidental.

Copyright © 2023 by Tim Wahl

All rights reserved. No part of this book may be reproduced or transmitted in any form or by any means, electronic or mechanical, including photocopying, recording, or by any information storage and retrieval system, or otherwise without the prior written permission from the author (registered trademark).

Cover art "Lucifer vs. Dragon" by Tiziana Ruiu

Copyright © 1-12507293341

Edited by Frank Wahl and Tim Wahl

Cataloging-in-Publication Data is on file with the Library of Congress.

ISBN: 9798391772347

Tim Wahl published this 2nd edition.

"Printed in the United States of America"
"April 2023"

Guardians of Paradise

by

Tim Wahl

Thanks page:

My mom and dad, Frank and Barb.

And to my Uncle and Godfather, Jim Kostlan (RIP), who showed me generosity, compassion, and love.

This book is dedicated to Azrael.

The Map of Aeiriel

Angel Characters of Heaven's Wars

Amy –whose name means the beloved. Long black hair, hourglass figure, and olive skin.

Azrael – first pupil of the Seven, whose name means whom God helps. Pure Seraphim. Long dirty blond hair with braids, pure muscle, and blue eyes.

Hapozetael – see **Opal Eye**

Israfel – high-ranking Seraphim angel, a messenger of the Seven. Whose name means the burning one. Long light brown hair with a petite frame but very defined.

Jrindren – high-ranking Seraphim angel. Has short sandy-blond hair and a thin but defined build

Lilith – high-ranking Seraphim and Cherubim. Long blond hair and white wings.

Opal Eye – real name, Hapozetael, mentor to Azrael, the eighth angel of creation, record keeper of Aeirliel.

Creatures and terms of Heaven's Wars

Aeirliel- The angel's term for the Garden of Eden.

Dragons- A giant bat-winged magical lizard. There are six types of dragons: Fire, Air, Earth, Water, Magic (art), and Shön. The Shön possesses all five elements and is the most powerful of the dragons. The dragon queen is the head of the society.

Fey- Six-inch humanoids with insect wings. They possess magical abilities and live in tropical areas. Bien is the king of the fey.

Griffin- A magical creature that is half eagle and half lion. From its waist up, it is an eagle, and the other half is a lion. Ina is the Matriarch of Griffin society.

Jinn- Magical humanoids cousins to the angels but with no wings.

Maeraz- A magical particle absorbed by magical beings. This is a unit of measurement that allows beings to use either heavenly or earthly magic.

Mermaids- A water-dwelling magical creature. The upper torso is that of a woman, and the lower torso is that of a fish. There are mermen, but the Matron Mother leads the society.

Phoenix- A magical bird that is known for rising from the ashes. They are bright in appearance and are capable of igniting fire around their bodies.

Unicorns- a horse with a single horn. They are magical and known for their healing abilities.

Hierarchy of the Angels

Ranks of the Heavenly Seven

1. **Lucifer** – the first angel and being created, whose name means bearer of light or light bearer, leader of all angels: white wings, long straight blond hair, muscular build, and green eyes.

2. **Michael** – the second angel created, whose name means who is like God: white wings, long straight golden hair, muscular build, and blue eyes.

3. **Gabriel** – the third angel created, whose name means the voice of God. The most versed in the laws of the Heavens. One of the most powerful Heavenly magic users in the Heavens. White wings, blond hair, well-built with white wings. Pure Cherubim.

4. **Beelzebub** – fourth angel created, whose name means the darkest light. White skin, long black hair, dark brown eyes, athletic build, and black wings. One of the strongest earthly magic users and one of the greatest swordsmen.

5. **Raphael** – the fifth angel created, whose name means whom God heals. Brown hair, blue eyes, and white wings. Expert healer and well-versed in Heavenly magic.

6. **Uriel** – the sixth angel created, whose name means the Fire of God. Red hair, green eyes, and red-feathered wings. One of the greatest swordsmen and the best archer in the Heavens.

7. **Zachriel** – the seventh angel created, whose name means the memory of God. Brown hair, brown eyes, and brown wings. Well-versed in the history of the universe and Heavenly Magic.

Nine choirs of angels

1. Seraphim
2. Cherubim
3. Thrones
4. Virtues
5. Powers
6. Dominions
7. Principalities
8. Archangels
9. Angels

Preface

God created Lucifer before all things to have a companion who would watch him create everything. He wanted to share and show everything to Lucifer. It is said that God even showed him the secrets of creation. As such, he wanted Lucifer to be perfect and did not want his first creation destroyed.

God made the firstborn dragons upon the creation of the Heavens and worlds. Each element was given a pair of dragons, male, and female. The five elements are Fire, Water, Earth, Air, and Magic. God also combined the elements and made four dragons from them. They would be known as shön and contained all the elements. Soon after, they and their direct descendants were known as the royal bloodline of the dragons. God would create many more dragons after the fourteen firstborns. Soon, the firstborns would also spawn more dragons of their own making. The dragon race was stout and fierce by nature. Their numbers became vast in a short period. In addition to the dragons, He made griffins who were not as powerful as the dragons but were like cousins. While God created more beings and worlds, he realized his creation, Lucifer, would also need companions.

Then God first made the angels. Like an artist seeking to refine his perfect creation, Lucifer, God made slight adjustments to the angel that followed him, Michael. He continued this process with the following seven angels of creation. Just as the griffins followed the creation of the dragons, the jinn came after the angels. They were like angels without wings. They had similar characteristics but were lesser in power. The jinn were cousins to the angels, much like the griffins being cousins to the dragons. Then like a star shattering into billions of pieces, he created billions of angels all at once.

With his kingdom made and beings created, God would pause before he continued to add to his vastness and glory. Such a time would be a blink to God, but to his subjects, it would be a long time. Peace would be challenging to keep within such time, jealousy would stir, and the First War would begin.

As the population of the dragons and griffins increased, they expanded their territories throughout the Garden of Eden or Aeirliel, as was known to angels. They became restless and desired more than just their areas of Eden. They eyed the many levels of the Heavens. Thus, they invaded the third Heaven. The angels and jinn fought back the invaders. While no victor was clear, the dragons and griffins established a new territory and sought to expand it.

The angels held the ground, but it was not easy. The numbers of dragons were vast, and they were, on average, more powerful than an average angel. While Uriel and other angels secured the area, the dragons shifted their gaze to the next Heaven. They did not need the entire third Heaven; they wanted to be a part of it. Their goal was to have a piece of each of the heavens. God did not want this, and the angels and jinn defended each of the Heavens.

The First War would be the first of many to come. Later, the angels would know the series of Wars as the Dragon Wars.

Introduction

In the great void of nothingness, God said, "Let there be light," and that light was Lucifer. Lucifer was created before time itself. He was the first of the many angels. Angels were the first creature made in God's image and the first of many other humanoid-shaped beings. God gave each of his angels feathered wings. The angels were ageless, and as they reached the peak of their body's perfection, they remained that way forever—unless a dragon or griffin struck them down by sword or fire or any other deadly force. Lucifer had been with God and knew how He had created each being. It was rumored that He even told him the secrets of creation. God gave the angels and other select beings He created at that time two forms of magic: Heavenly—used primarily for defense and protection— and Earthly—used to attack and destroy. Each angel favored one form of magic.

God loved His first creation and never wanted Lucifer to be destroyed. To ensure that, He made him the strongest of all angels; his wounds healed faster than any who came after him. Many believed him to be God's most powerful creation. Lucifer was far older than any of his angelic brothers and sisters. He was thought by many to be indestructible and unkillable. No matter how many centuries elapsed, Lucifer and the other angels appeared in their twenties, although they could alter their appearance in age or form when they wished. The first seven angels were adults from their first breath. As God created more angels, they had two years of childhood and then reached adulthood. The six angels who came after Lucifer were Michael, Gabriel, Beelzebub, Raphael, Uriel, and Zachriel. They were known as the Heavenly Seven—the seven princes of the Heavens—and were the leaders of God's angels. God gave them a pupil to instruct.

Azrael was the first and only pupil of the Seven. He was considered one of the smallest Seraphim angels created in height and build. They trained him, especially in the magics, combat and knowledge of the universe, to prepare him for a destiny that would prove to be more important than anyone could imagine. He held within himself great potential to rise in the angels' ranks and someday be equal in strength to Lucifer. Because of these reasons and many others, he would be the only angel directly made by God to be a pupil of the Seven. His destiny would be strung together with Lucifer's in a way that would affect the entire universe.

In the beginning, God generated worlds and beings to inhabit them at an accelerated rate. Angels were the one creation that He forbade to procreate or kiss. But they were also the only ones permitted to live permanently in His perfect Heavens. He made a world known as Aeirliel, the Garden of Eden or Paradise. That world was connected to the other Heavens. The creatures in it were like angels; they did not age or die from an illness. Because that world was so close to the Heavens, the angels were involved in its operation more than any other place in the universe. God held them accountable for keeping peace and order amongst those that dwelt there. One of the creature types was the dragons; they were by far the most powerful creatures in Paradise and all of creation.

Verinity, queen of the dragons, believed that the dragons deserved to be a part of the Heavens, as the angels were. The dragons thought they were the most powerful of all God's creatures. Because of their greed and arrogance, they instigated a series of battles against the angels. These skirmishes lasted for many millennia, with brief periods of peace in between.

But another creation threatened an even greater war.

God forged a world called Earth that was immensely larger than Aeirliel. It was on a separate plane of existence. He created a being to manage and control it; she was Mother Earth. She commanded the elements and spoke to all the living creatures. God wished to spawn a new creation made of parts of Himself and the Earth. Upon this creation, evil would be born.

From this point, a timeless battle between good and evil ensued that would be fought throughout the ages and this is how it began…

Chapter 1

The sky was a surreal brown. The air smelled of death and the winds roared in chaos. In the world of Aeirliel, in the area called Gethyn, the ground could not be seen through dark gray clouds of smoke. The blood of dragons and angels covered the terrain. The corpses of both species lay everywhere. The horror scene displayed was not the typical beauty of the canyon of Gethyn.

The angels that weren't too weak to fly fled in terror from their dragon adversaries. Those who were able carried the injured. Dragons hovered in the sky, covering the ground with a thick blanket of deadly firepower. Some could shoot lightning, fire, cold or acid from their mouths; others, magic blasts that exploded and injured or killed many of the angels. The dragons were like wolves pursuing sheep.

While the angels had the advantage of numbers against their foes, they were no match for the size of this dragon force. A formation of angels fled through a canyon with a colossal dragon in pursuit, shooting fire. At the telepathic command, the formation deftly broke off in different directions, and the heavenly soldiers turned as one and shot blasts of ice at the dragon's wings. The beast could not slow down in time and smashed into the canyon wall.

Other angels were not so fortunate. With a lust for a kill, a vicious shön dragon—the size of a killer whale and flying as gracefully as the whale swims in water—hunted down his enemies. Shön dragons were the most powerful of all dragons. They were masters of all five elements, fire, water, earth, air and art (or magic). First, it picked off the injured, crushing them with its claws or crunching them between its teeth. A few brave angels shot arrows into its thick hide but had no effect. The agile monster maneuvered out of harm's way, then shot a cone of ice, freezing the top half of his winged adversaries. As it passed them, it whipped its tail at them, and they shattered to pieces.

The angels continued their retreat down the canyon, trying to reach a safe place to regroup. As they fled in chaos, there was no hope for them. Some could launch spells to fight back, but they were only strong enough to kill smaller dragons. It was not enough. As the dim light of hope wavered like a candle about to go out, the shepherd who guided the sheep arrived.

Lucifer screamed as he cut across the sky incredibly fast, charging headlong toward the shön dragon. The colossal creature heard him and altered its course from the group of angels it was pursuing toward the bigger prize. Other dragons saw Lucifer and fled while a brave or foolish few shifted their course in his direction. Lucifer's presence cheered the angels. Now the sheep would bite back at the wolves.

Lucifer led the dragon through the gray smoke and mist that covered the ground into a screaming ascent that pierced the surreal brown sky. He banked left and fired white balls of energy at the beast. It tucked in its wings as it drew closer to him. Two white energy balls missed, but one hit the dragon's wing and slowed it down. The leader of the angels charged, gripping his shimmering claymore sword tightly. The shön dragon shot multiple lines of magic from its talons. Lucifer held out his free hand and commanded a green energy ward, which acted as a shield, to deflect the power surges.

The giant shön dragon raised its head and revealed a mouth full of sharp teeth and foul breath. It snapped at Lucifer, but the angel was too quick. In an instant, Lucifer slid away and cut the dragon across the neck. The wound was deep but not fatal and the shön dragon escaped a possible second wound from his attacker. Lucifer moved past it to greet the horde of oncoming dragons who craved a chance to kill the legendary angel.A fire dragon tried to scorch him, but Lucifer pushed his

3

sword up and under its throat. A breath of fire burst up into the sky. Lucifer quickly smashed his mighty fist into the dragon's head, which spun thirty yards away. As the battle raged on, Lucifer continued his magnificent display of strength and skill. One dragon after another fell to him. Some scraped or clawed him, but his wounds mended in seconds. Some creatures made a second attempt to dethrone the king of the sky. However, the result was the same. The defeated serpents of the sky returned to the canyon floor, either in death or by their own choice. The tales throughout the dragon clans that Lucifer's strength was equal to that of an ancient dragon were not exaggerated.

The winged shepherd floated alone in the sky, taking in his victory without a scratch. He dove through the gray clouds and began his quest to rally his brothers and sisters. Although the skirmish was at a momentary end, they would need to regroup.

"Quickly, through the canyon!" he ordered, speaking directly to their minds.

The remaining angels ran or flew as fast as they could, some carrying the last wounded stragglers from the battlefield. Lucifer covered their retreat as they fled. He alternated between a steady barrage of lightning and small energy blasts to discourage any dragons from following. Other angels assisted his efforts. After all, this was not his fight alone, but he always carried himself as if he were the only hope of victory.

Finally, the fleeing angels reached a fortified position. Angels lined up along the canyon walls and down the trench, just as Lucifer had instructed. Any dragons bloodthirsty enough to attack became prey. From this vantage point, the angels were the hunters and the dragons, the prey. Balls of fire wreaked havoc on the dragons' onslaught, although the fire and shön dragons were immune. The angels' arrows and magical spells covered the sky. Well-placed spears pierced the dragons through their open mouths, killing them instantly. The wave of dragons crashed against the wall of angels. The two forces held their ground, with neither side gaining a distinct advantage. Once again, Lucifer would try to be the difference maker.

He had swooped down to protect wounded angels from the horse-sized dragons who could easily penetrate their ranks. Lucifer caught a dragon in midair and threw it into its comrades, knocking them aside. They shot acid at him, and again he blocked it with a green energy ward. Another beast approached him from his left flank. Luckily, another angel saw the dragon and stepped in front of the fire projected at Lucifer.

"Lucifer!" the angel shouted a warning.

As he turned, Lucifer saw the other angel covered in fire. He quickly put out the flames, even while he caught on fire. An angel called Israfel swooped in with a squadron of angels to aid Lucifer and the fallen angel. Their immediate impact made the area safe, at least for the moment. Lucifer knelt beside the burnt angel. Lucifer's wounds mended as he assessed the angel.

"Hold on, my brother," Lucifer urged him.

Lucifer started to heal the soldier's wounds but was interrupted by a touch on his shoulder.

"Lucifer, the Father has called you and the other Seven to an important meeting. He sent me to tell you to return to the palace as soon as possible," Israfel told him.

Lucifer narrowed his eyes with a hint of frustration. He did not want to leave. He wanted to remain with his brothers and sisters. But the Father called upon him, and there was nothing more important to him than serving God.

The angel on the ground turned his head. "I will be all right, my brother."

"I am sorry I must leave like this," Lucifer apologized.

Israfel stepped forward. "I shall tend to him. Please go, brother."

Lucifer rose and nodded. "Be well, my brothers and sisters. I swear I will return with more angels to aid you."

Lucifer sprang into the air, heading for a white portal that Israfel and the angels had passed through in the sky. Portals were only used to crossover to different planes or dimensions. They were never put up in the middle of combat because of the risk and danger to allies. Lucifer entered, and the portal closed behind him.

Chapter 2

Light burst throughout the Heavens, which contained a massive and glorious kingdom. Buildings made of marble, ivory, opal, and stones unknown on Earth shimmered across the kingdom from end to end—a mosaic of white, cream, pale lavender, and pastel blue. All reflected the shades of the vast golden sky and the floating clouds. A bright light shone everywhere, without a source. Its cool blue hue saturated the environment. The walls were cold and rounded as though shaped by water. God's light always shone, touching everything in the Heavens, making the kingdom's streams, rivers and waterfalls radiant and refreshing. The trees and plant life resonated with the smooth texture of the buildings. The trees contained small white flowers as soft as silk and stretched high into the sky.

Angels soared above the city, serene and at ease. Some rode winged horses and others guided the flying animals from their perch on golden chariots. Below them, at the center of the vast city, stood the Palace of the Seven.

The palace was the crown jewel in a city of perfection. It was surrounded by water at the base and was over hundred kilometers in diameter. It was made of robust and sturdy ivory and white marble. Many towers rose from the vast base of the building. Each slender, circular tower narrowed to a sharp point at the top. One tower stood higher than any other pinnacle in the city.

A shooting star cut across the sky. As it neared the palace, it slowed, revealing the angel Lucifer. He landed softly on an upper balcony and folded his white-feathered wings into his back. He was dressed in his battle attire but wore no armor. His loose garments were brown, green, and white; his arms were exposed and his chest was partially bare. He entered the palace and walked down a curved corridor toward the council room of the Heavenly Seven.

Lucifer opened the door and saw his six younger brothers: Michael, Gabriel, Beelzebub, Raphael, Uriel, and Zachriel. All wore casual white clothes except for Beelzebub, who wore black and white, and Uriel, who wore no shirt. The two had been assigned to lead legions of angels in other areas of Aeirliel, while the other four had been instructed to rest and mend their wounds. Lucifer had told them that even the heavenly seven needed to rest every once in a while.

The circular room in which they sat was completely white. Marble pillars formed an inner circle where seven stone chairs faced one another. There was no head chair, and each was the same size as the others. Despite the varying ranks of the Seven, each had an equal voice, and therefore no place was grander than another. But because each brother was unique, each chair had been designed to fit his personality.

Michael was the first to greet the newcomer. "Glad you could join us," he said with a welcoming smile. "We were afraid you would not make it."

"When Father calls upon me, I always come with the greatest of haste, even when we are in the middle of a war," Lucifer declared.

"What news do you bring of your current battle?" Beelzebub interjected with curiosity.

Lucifer paused, closed his green eyes, and sighed softly. His thoughts went to the faces of the brothers and sisters fighting beside him. The angels he had sworn to look after and protect with all his heart and strength. Then he saw each of them die—some in his arms, others protecting him from a fatal blow and falling at his side. He tried everything in his power to keep them all alive and prevent any harm from coming to them, but it never seemed to be enough. No matter what he did, some of his siblings died and would continue to do so. And when an angel died, they ceased to exist."It continues with great cost to both sides," he forced himself to reply. "Aeirliel is no longer the paradise Father intended it to be."

The firmly built Uriel placed a hand on his shoulder. "I am sure with you there to lead them, the cost was far less than it would have been otherwise," he said with an encouraging smile.

Placing an angel's hand on another's shoulder was a sign of respect or mentorship. In this case, it was Uriel's way of showing respect to his older brother.

"I will go back with you," Raphael proclaimed. "I will be able to heal most of our brothers and sisters before they even realize they have a wound."

Uriel narrowed his eyes. "If you go, then I will follow. We do not need you being a hero as you did in the last battle."

The angels all smiled and chuckled at the memory. Raphael cared only for the safety of those around him and nothing for himself. He had taken six arrows in a previous battle as he healed wounded angels before Uriel finally forced him to stop.

"I was only hit by a few times," Raphael objected.

"A few times? You looked like a porcupine by the time Uriel and I reached you. Thankfully, we were not wounded, or else you might have insisted on healing us too," Zachriel spoke with complete accuracy.

Again the Seven smiled, remembering the great battle and the many angels who owed their lives to Raphael's healing skills.

Quirking an eyebrow, Raphael settled back in his chair. "Since when did you two develop a sense of humor?"

"I learned it from you," Uriel answered.

"And here I thought it was me. But I am a modest fellow." Beelzebub smirked with delight.

"Have you all become comedians while nursing your wounds?" Lucifer asked with a chuckle.

"See what you have been missing, big brother," the shy Michael whispered.

Just then, a bright warm light filled the room. At the center of the light, a humanoid figure appeared. It was God. He was taller than all of the Seven. He was elderly in appearance. He had long white hair and a white beard that reached His chest. An aura appeared around Him and he was slightly transparent. His loving blue eyes gazed into the souls of the angels. They knelt before Him.

"Rise, My Heavenly Seven," God commanded. "Please sit down."

They took their seats, and God calmly walked around the center of the room.

"I brought you here to tell you that I intend to add a being to the land of Aeirliel. It will be unique—different from anything else I have made."

"What kind of being?" Lucifer queried. He was upset that he had been asked to leave his brothers and sisters dying on the battlefield for this announcement. But he quieted those feelings and listened to his Father.

"They will be similar to you, my angels, created in My image, as all of you were. I will create them not only from Myself but also from the Earth. They will not be able to use any of the magics. They will be called humans and mortal in mind and body."

"Will they be placed on Earth?" Gabriel asked.

"No, I want them to be in Aeirliel, My Paradise, closer to us. But I will need seven pinches of the Earth's soil to create the first human. The soil must come from a place near the

Water of Eternal Youth. I know that a great war rages on, but because of this creation, a time of peace and prosperity will come. Who will do this task for me?"

"I will volunteer," both Michael and Gabriel responded.

Uriel stood. "And I will join them."

"The three of you may attempt this, but before you go, know that Mother Earth will give you three trials to obtain her soil. She may not give the soil to you freely. Do what you feel should be done to obtain this soil."

Gabriel glanced at Michael. "What are the trials?"

"They will test your wit, your strength, and your heart," God responded.

"Surely, one of us will be able to pass." Uriel was very confident.

"Lucifer, I know the war is taking a heavy toll on you and all the angels. What must be done to give everyone peace?" God inquired.

"We must use all the angels that are willing and able. With the griffins now aiding the dragons, their numbers are too great. It may take more than just the angels," Lucifer explained.

"This war has gone on far too long, Father," Beelzebub added.

"So many have perished on both sides. Beelzebub," God observed.

"Beelzebub, assemble legions of reinforcements to come with me. Help me end this war." Lucifer pleaded to his younger brother.

"I will gather as many as I can. A legion in Aeirliel has secured its position," Beelzebub assured, lowering his head and tilting it slightly.

"What about me? I may be of help," Raphael suggested.

God smiled, pleased with His angelic children's eagerness to help do the right thing. These seven angels were special to Him. He knew He had done well in making them.

"Raphael can help mend the wounded, as he always does. Thank you, My Seven. My time for rest will come, but I will continue creating and adding more to this universe. Be well, My children." God dematerialized in a bright flash of light.

The Seven turned to one another and then looked to Lucifer.

"I promised to return with another legion of angels," Lucifer broke the silence.

"Then you will return with three," Beelzebub assured him.

"Others are training that would go with you," Michael said.

Lucifer began to think out loud. "Perhaps I can help them with their training before we go."

"Don't you mean to make an inspiring spectacle of yourself?" Raphael joked.

Lucifer winked. "Perhaps."

Chapter 3

Earth was covered in endless lush green terrain and a clear blue ocean surrounding a solid land mass. There were high, jagged mountains and sloping green valleys. Fields of wildflowers in brilliant yellow, purple, orange, and pink contrasted with undulating beige sands. In the tundra regions, the climate was ice-cold, frozen and barren; in the desert, the sun beat down, scorching the sand. In the forests and valleys, the cool breezes blew, riffling the leaves and grasses and the vibrant petals of the flowers. The massive body of land was more than three times the size of Aeirliel and was surrounded by water. Magical animals and those without magic inhabited the land to the ends of the Earth.

In one of these landscapes stood an angel named Azrael. He looked around the tropical garden of trees and silk-soft grass and took a deep breath. The air was clean and moist from the morning's dew. The trees had thick, round trunks and the branches stretched out like arms over the ground, providing shade. Around the trees were bushes with profuse green leaves. Azrael adored the sights and sounds of nature and its numerous animals.

He was in his early twenties, six-foot-one with an athletic frame, but his body was pure muscle. He wore his long, wavey blond hair with a few strands braided as it passed over his shoulders. From his waist hung a wide belt with twin curved blades on his left side. His clothes were light, thin, and soft to the touch, but they kept him warm as they hugged his body. He wore the angel's standard white, black and gold attire. A symbol of a small sun appeared on his chest. His light azure eyes gazed at the angels that surrounded him.

"Earth is designed like Aeirliel, though it is on a different plane of existence. But time is much different there. The days

14

on Earth are 24 hours long, while Aeirliel's are 36 hours. Creations on Earth age over time and become frail, which does not happen in Aeirliel," Azrael explained to his fellow angels.

"What are our duties to the Earth?" an angel named Maktiel asked.

"All life forms in this world serve a purpose and are linked to one another. It will be your task to keep them balanced." A white rose materialized in Azrael's hand behind his back, and he showed it to the angels. "There are many different species of plants and animals; your first task must be to learn their characteristics and how they interact."

"I want you to explore this world and return with something similar to what I showed you. Please bring it to our next gathering. That will be all for today. Be well."

The angels unfolded their wings and flew away. Azrael looked at the white rose and smiled as he thought of the many roses he had given to Amy, his closest friend. He gave them to her because he felt she was like a white rose. Her features were as soft and beautiful as the petals of a rose. While she might be delicate in appearance, she would stand up for herself and pierce your skin, as would the thorn of a rose. The white of the rose represented her purity and innocence. Though the thought of her always brought a smile to his face, it saddened him to know they would never be together as he truly wanted. It was painful to keep his love and passion for her a secret.

Azrael held one of his hands out and a gateway shaped like a sphere formed before him. The floating portal shimmered like water in the air. Azrael stepped through, and it immediately closed behind him.

****

Books, scrolls, and components for spells crammed the sagging shelves in the quarters of Hapozetael. Dim lights floated in the air throughout the room. Additional smaller lights danced around the room, but they were actually small creatures called Fey. The Fey dressed in very revealing clothing and lived on a tropical island. The females had a reputation for being extremely flirtatious, which is why several of the Fey king's daughters were under his care.

The angel Hapozetael sat at his desk in his home in the land of Aeirliel and stroked his gray and white beard. He wore a thick baize robe that touched the floor. The sleeves hung loosely at his wrists, and his robes hung over his small framed body. One of his eyes had been replaced with an opal gemstone. The opal stone held magical properties that enabled him to see things that his angelic eye would not. This gave him the nickname Opal Eye, which most called him. He was the only angel who had chosen to age in his appearance as time passed. He stood at five-feet-eight inches, but in his proper and youthful form, he was six-foot-six and had hair as black as night. He was the eighth angel of creation, and one of the few angels made as an adult. Other angels were allowed to experience childhood for two years.

Sitting across from him was a beautiful angel named Amy. She wore a spaghetti-strap white dress that exposed her hourglass shape. Her skin was a dark olive color and was smooth and cool to the touch. Her long, wavy, black hair flowed down her back and curled at the end of her petite body. Her eyes were a golden brown, filled with innocence and delight. She was small in height, but her heart was large and full of joy and happiness. She wrote furiously as Opal Eye talked.

"Close the book, Amy. Now!" Opal Eye bellowed, hitting the table with his gnarled fist.

Amy quickly complied.

"Tell me the order of the nine choirs from highest to lowest." Opal Eye waited.

"Seraphim, Cherubim, Thrones, and…uhh…the next one I can never remember." Amy bit her lip with nervousness.

"Virtues, Amy. This is simple Angelic order. I wonder how you do not know this, given that you are a Seraphim." Opal Eye sighed with frustration.

"Seraphim is the most powerful. Right?" she asked.

"They are supposed to be and as a general rule, yes. Maybe God forgot about that when He made you."

Amy looked hurt.

"Come now, child, you know I think highly of you," Opal Eye changed his tone. "I see within you immense strength and power."

Amy smiled and was energized. "Why do we have the nine choirs?"

"Questions, questions," Opal Eye chided.

"How else am I going to learn?"

"By remembering the answer the first time," the old angel retorted. "Now let's review the nine choirs and who represents each choir to form the council of the nine. We will review some of the basic spells of Heavenly magic and Earthly magic. You must understand that while these forms have some of the same spells, they may not have the same potency or be more difficult to cast. For example, Heavenly healing spells tend to be stronger than Earthly and are easier to cast for someone who favors that form of magic. While Earthly magic can cast a spell—"

Opal Eye continued to speak, but his student's attention was already on other things. She observed some fey women casting spells that made flowers appear out of thin air. She saw them morph into mice and rabbits and smiled. Those were the spells she wanted to learn. She had no desire to learn how to make wards or protection, lightning bolts, or any other spells leading to them. It was the simple things in life that she enjoyed. She wanted to live her life from moment to moment and not worry about what lay ahead for her in the future. She wanted to experience life and enjoy what was around her. But as a Seraphim, she had far more responsibilities, duties, and obligations than others.

Amy saw one of the fey women create a small white light within her hands. She could expand and contract the size of the white energy at will. The white light would move around her arms and body with ease. She was fascinated by the spell and tried to do as the fey. She reached within the core of her soul and softly chanted the words she had heard the fey speak. The light appeared in her hands. It was warm and flared as Amy moved it slowly in her hands under the desk. She smiled, and the light grew in her hands, but she did not know how or why it did. It started to burn the desk. She didn't know what to do to stop the spell. She tried closing her hands around the white orb, but it expanded even more when she opened them again. Smoke started to rise from her burning desk.

Opal Eye continued to write on his board as he lectured, but he stopped when his nose caught wind of the smoke in his chambers. He used the magic in the opal stone eye and saw what he could not see with his back turned. He wrinkled his nose and sniffed a few times before turning to Amy.

"What is this? Casting spells during my lecture?!" he grumbled.

Amy gasped and dropped the ball of white light, but it did not fall on the ground. Opal Eye caught the orb using telekinesis. He produced small flakes of ice to douse the fire beneath the desk with his other hand. He moved the sphere in front of Amy.

"Now hold it between your hands and repeat these words," he instructed his young student in Angelic. She complied, and the orb shrank and disappeared.

"Tell me, my young student, where did you learn to cast this simple but very dangerous spell?" he questioned.

Amy glanced around the room. The fey quickly hid in corners and holes throughout the room.

"I see. I shall have words with you all later," he shouted as the fey cringed in their hiding places. "But as for you, Amy, you cannot cast such a spell without knowing what you are doing. Do you know what damage this spell can cause?"

"No," Amy admitted.

"All the more reason you should not be casting it," Opal Eye admonished her.

"But it looked like fun," Amy sighed.

"Fun, is it? Well then, I suppose I shall have you write me a scroll on how the spell works. I want the complete history, usage, and power behind that spell. I have enough to write about after your lessons. I do not need any more delays or distractions," Opal Eye decreed.

Amy sighed and wrote a note on a scroll in front of her. Azrael appeared in the room but in a spectral form. He did not make a sound or make his presence known.

"Why are you always writing the history of Aeirliel and the Heavens?" she asked.

Opal rubbed his eyes in aggravation. "More questions?"

"Can't someone give you a break for a while? Maybe then you wouldn't be so grumpy."

"Now, see here. We all have our duties. Mine is to write the history of Aeirliel, not the Heavens. Zachriel writes the history of the Heavens."

"Did you write that you use any excuse to be grumpy?" Amy huffed.

Azrael grinned and snickered.

"I am not grumpy," Opal Eye informed her. "Azrael, you can come out now."

Azrael phased into sight and bowed his head slightly toward Opal Eye.

"Azrael!" Amy cried in delight.

"Hello, Amy. Hello, Opal Eye."

Amy ran over to hug Azrael tightly. She buried her face in his chest as he returned the embrace. They looked at each other, and at that moment, they forgot about the world around them. They saw only each other as their hearts raced from a simple touch.

"It is so good to see you," she said finally.

"It is good to see you too," he replied.

Opal Eye cleared his throat. "In case you had not noticed, I was in the middle of a lesson. You remember lessons?"

"I am sorry, Opal Eye. I am sure she can learn this tomorrow. You see, today is her naming day," Azrael explained.

"You remembered!"

"Of course."

"Opal Eye didn't," Amy said.

"Of course," Azrael repeated, somewhat more wryly.

"Wait just a moment. Just because I did not say…." Opal Eye objected.

"I thought I could be your teacher for the remainder of today," Azrael suggested.

"I would like that." Amy turned to Opal Eye. "May I please go with him?"

Opal Eye rolled his eyes. "Consider it my gift to you."

Amy lit up with joy and turned back to Azrael. She was greeted with a white rose.

"For your naming day," he said.

She took it bashfully, closing her golden-brown eyes and inhaling its scent.

She smiled. "Thank you."

"You are welcome!" interrupted Opal Eye with his arms crossed.

Amy rushed over to hug him before she and Azrael left his chambers.

"Have you awakened your wings yet?" inquired Azrael.

She hung her head. "No, I'm too scared."

Azrael turned her to face him, searching her eyes carefully as he asked, "Is that truly the reason?"

She balked at the question, unable to meet his bright azure eyes. He knew it was more than her fears. She preferred that Azrael carried her in his arms when he flew. She loved being close to him and knew that if she could fly, she might no longer get that chance to be held in his arms. It was a feeling she did not want to let go.

Azrael unfolded his wings and held out his hand to her.

"Let me show you the world known as Earth."

Amy grasped his hand, and Azrael wrapped an arm around her. He waved his other hand, and after a time, a white portal opened a few feet above them. Amy held on to him, and he flew into the air with her in his arms through the portal to Earth.

Chapter 4

Light filled the sky and danced on the waterways flowing throughout the city of the Seventh Heaven—thousands of angels trained through the art of magic and combat. Angels were divided into four different groups: Earthly magic, Heavenly magic, ranged combat, and melee combat.

In the Earthly magic group, angels practiced various forms of destructive spells. Some of them used elements of nature, creating blue fire and large gusts of wind. Others used forms of magical energy that varied in color. The blue spark was in the shape of small round balls the size of a closed fist. The red energy shot out from the angel's hands in a line. The rest used forms of telekinesis to move objects, such as rocks and anvils.

The Heavenly magic group focused on spells of protection and defense, such as invisibility and illusion. Some angels fooled their opponents with copies of themselves; others scared them with the illusions of dragons, and some angels made defensive shields of energy to block attacks.

The archers and spearmen practiced firing their weapons on horseback and winged horses. In melee combat, the angels paired up and scrimmaged, using swords, shields, or spears made of wood. Lucifer, Beelzebub, and Raphael observed the training sessions. Four angels practicing with wooden swords went at half speed and did not take the training seriously. Lucifer frowned and stepped toward the group.

"Hold! Stop at once! I have seen enough. If you think you are properly prepared to fight a war with movements like those, you are mistaken," Lucifer informed them.

Lucifer picked up a wooden sword and twirled it. "I want the four of you to attack me. Do not hold back. Nothing less than the best you can do."

The angels looked at each other and readied their swords. They slowly moved around Lucifer and surrounded him. He had to be ready for an attack from all possible angles.

"Begin!" he shouted.

Lucifer quickly threw his sword directly at the angel in front of him. It struck him in the head, and the strength and speed of the blow knocked him unconscious. The remaining angels took that as their cue to strike, but Lucifer dodged each attempt from them. With a magnificent flip in the air, Lucifer sprang off the wall and picked up the wooden sword he had thrown at the now-unconscious angel. He countered attacks as he sped between his inexperienced foes, quickly encircling them. He slammed his fist into the stomach of one angel, and he dropped to his knees. He grabbed the same angel and flipped him over his back.

The remaining two angels launched a barrage of attacks at Lucifer. While a few hit him, he was unaffected, and others he blocked or dodged. One angel tried to strike him, but Lucifer's body faded from sight, and the sword passed right through where he once stood. He reappeared in solid form behind the trainee and whacked the angel to the ground. The last angel knew Lucifer could move swiftly, but he was astonished at his inability to keep up with the onslaught. Lucifer knocked the angel's sword from his hand and proceeded to strike the helpless soldier, but Beelzebub blocked his wooden blade with his sword.

"I think you have proven your point, my friend," Beelzebub rebuked him softly.

Lucifer nodded and dropped his blade.

Beelzebub helped one of the trainees to his feet while Raphael healed the angels' bumps and bruises.

"I am sorry if I was too hard on you, brothers," Lucifer told the still-stunned quartet. "But I refuse to send any more of you to your deaths. The Griffins and Dragons will be far more brutal to you than I. Beelzebub, please review with them how to properly hold a sword before we depart."

"Of course," Beelzebub bowed.

Chapter 5

Earth was like a newborn, filled with life, wonders, and curiosity. The planet was covered with warm, rich green grasses and trees, with crystal clear blue oceans that crashed along smooth shorelines. As endless as the land mass seemed, the sea was even more substantial.

Michael soared in the cloudless sapphire sky. He spotted Uriel and Gabriel standing near the Water of Eternal Youth and descended. "Were either of you able to complete the trials?" he asked.

"No," Uriel responded.

Gabriel shook his head. "Nor was I."

"I am sad to say the same," Michael sighed in defeat.

"We cannot return empty-handed," Gabriel urged them to continue trying.

"I agree. What is to stop us from taking the soil right now? For some reason, Mother Earth was pleased that I failed. I feel she had no intention of giving me what I came for, even if I did pass," Uriel reasoned.

Gabriel and Uriel looked at Michael for approval. He took a moment and thought about the next course of action. Were any of them meant to do this? Without question, one of the Heavenly Seven was meant for it. Lucifer would be the most logical choice. If none of them were meant to get the soil, then why would God have asked them in the first place? Maybe it was not a task meant for them, but they were to find the one destined for this path. "I agree we should try, but I believe she has no intention of giving it to us. Maybe this is not for us to complete. Maybe it is for another."

"If not one of us, then who?" Gabriel asked.

"I do not have an answer, but maybe we should regroup and meet with the rest of the Seven," he suggested.

"We came here to do this, and the Water of Eternal Youth is right before us," Gabriel stretched out his arm.

The three angels approached the edge of the Water of Eternal Youth.

Uriel stepped in front of Gabriel and Michael. "Nothing to fear. All is quiet." Uriel moved before his two older brothers and confidently stepped to the water's edge.

"That is what worries me." Michael drew his sword and shield.

Gabriel quietly chanted a spell while Uriel kneeled and pulled out a small brown pouch. He took a pinch of soil and dropped it in the bag. "I told you, nothing to worry about," Uriel shrugged.

An immense shadow covered the three angels.

"Uriel, slowly put the soil back on the ground," Michael commanded.

Uriel looked up and saw a chimera, a massive creature with three heads: a dragon, a maneless lion, and a griffin. The chimera was giant in height and towered over the trees. Muscles bulged in its legs as each head roared. Smoke sizzled out of the dragon's nose. The lion's head drooled as it eyed its prey. Each drop of drool could have overflowed a bathtub. The griffin head shrieked and the chimera swiped, hitting Uriel with its claw. The blow sent the angel flying into a tree trunk and he dropped the soil. The chimera's heads roared as it lifted into the air flapping its leathery wings. Gabriel shot a blast of blue energy at the beast, and it tumbled back to the ground. Michael quickly leaped toward the chimera, slicing his sword through the air at the beast. He attempted to wound it, but it deflected his blows.

With ease, Uriel lifted himself to his feet using his wings. He was surrounded at once by earth elementals. Each of the earth elementals varied in size and shape. Made of stone, they were each distinctive, from a pointy shale creature reaching

Uriel's shoulder to a smaller, rounder version made of smooth river rock towering over him. Uriel pulled out his twin swords and whirled them in front, around, and along his body. He somersaulted over five of his enemies while cutting off their heads. He quickly carved up four more earth elementals by slicing their arms and legs off. He massacred any that dared to challenge him. Uriel's movements were quick and precise. He bested each earth elemental within two or three moves. As soon as he incapacitated them, they crumbled at his feet. He spun his blades around his back and sliced a final foe in half.

"Is that the best you can throw at me?" he called.

Over fifty earth elementals popped up from the ground all around him. Water elementals emerged from the nearby pool to join them. Uriel gave a poised smile and whirled his blades. "Now that's better."

He sprang into action and moved with incredible speed among his gathered adversaries. He hacked through dozens of the rock men, cutting off legs and arms. He disabled or destroyed any he struck. He chanted a few words, and his blades ignited with blue fire. He sliced at the water elements, and they evaporated into the air.

Elementals could take any shape they wished. They would typically not be an exact copy of the creature they would copy. They could shape themselves with two arms or four arms and two legs or four legs or wings. They were composed of the same element they were forged from: fire, water, air or earth. Their appearance ranges from a wingless angel of air to a fire horse.

The chimera shot fire from the dragon's mouth at Michael, but Gabriel quickly cast a spell that created a green energy shield around him and blocked the fire. Michael unfurled his gleaming white wings and sprang into the air with a shout. He propelled himself upward, gliding with the wind. Michael wove in and around the chimera, avoiding strikes from its claws and the snapping teeth of three heads. He slashed it across the chest and maneuvered to cut off one of its heads, but it smashed him to the ground with one of its deadly claws.

Gabriel reached toward the chimera, reciting a spell, and an electric charge powered around his fingers and palm. As a lightning bolt surged from his hand, an earth elemental struck him from behind. He fell but managed to spin in midair before hitting the ground. He knocked the earth elemental to the ground with his staff. Gabriel landed on his knees, but numerous earth elementals surrounded him as he tried to stand Arrows exploded through the craniums of five earth elementals, destroying them all. From his vantage point, hovering ten feet above the ground, Uriel continued to fire arrows with blinding speed and deadly accuracy.

"Uriel! Help Michael!" Gabriel commanded

Michael was pinned on the ground by the Chimera and could not find an opening among the thundering blows of the three-headed beast. Uriel set his aim in Michael's direction, but a water elemental caught his leg and pulled him toward the army of attackers. Uriel was forced to protect himself and fired arrows firing at the creatures that tried to bring him to the ground.

Michael rolled away from the fire of the Chimera, only slightly singed. The griffin's sharp beak snapped down, but Michael escaped again. He was forced to roll left and right from the non-stop attacks of the three heads. The beak of the griffin finally cut him. Michael grimaced in pain and grabbed his flesh-torn shoulder. The Chimera saw its opportunity and moved to chop down on the injured angel with sharp dragon teeth.

Suddenly, Lucifer appeared and sliced off the Chimera's dragonhead. It fell feebly to an Earth that was shattered from the conflict.

Michael looked up and met Lucifer's eyes, nodding in gratitude. Lucifer returned the gesture with a smirk as he hurled balls of white energy at the chimera and forced it away from Michael. The chimera was overwhelmed and weakened from the loss of the head. It retreated into the forest.

Lucifer landed next to Michael and helped him to his feet. Before they could speak, a gigantic mass of creatures composed of all four of the Earth's elements hurdled toward the angels. Uriel landed between Lucifer and Michael, and with a deep breath, he unleashed another onslaught of arrows at the creatures. Michael and Lucifer readied their swords and moved to Uriel's flanks to cover him.

When Gabriel saw the massive force, a hint of irritation crossed his face, and the hues of his eyes ignited and flared to a faint blue and white. He murmured the few words of a spell, and a white light appeared in his hand. As he clapped his hands together, the wind roared against his face. The white-hot energy, once the size of his hand, expanded rapidly to the magnitude of a vast mountain. The sphere of energy encompassed the elemental forces and incinerated all of them. It was the same spell Opal Eye had warned Amy about.

Gabriel leaned on his staff to give himself support; he was exhausted from the force he had used to cast the spell. Such energy use was taxing, even to an angel as mighty as Gabriel.

"Return to the Kingdom. This task is not meant for any of us," Lucifer assured them.

They all entered the small portal Lucifer had come through and left open. They all disappeared, leaving only the quiet pool behind.

Chapter 6

The sun danced on the sea as waves smoothly collapsed upon the shore. Azrael and Amy walked on the wet sand in their bare feet.

Azrael gazed out at the ocean and took a deep breath of the moist air. He loved looking at the water—waterfalls, rivers, or the undulating sea. But the ocean always gave him a sense of peace and tranquility. He turned and looked at Amy. He could not think of anywhere he would prefer to be but now and in this place.

"Is every place on Earth as beautiful as this?" she asked.

"There are others. I wanted to show you one of my favorites first."

"What about the creatures here? Are they similar to those of Aeirliel?" Amy looked around in rapt wonder.

"Some are the same. Some only exist here, and some only there."

"Show me one of them, Azrael. Please?"

They stopped walking, and Azrael stepped in front of her. They looked at each other briefly before Azrael broke the connection with a gentle smile. He put his hand on her shoulder and pointed. She turned her head and gasped. Behind her was a herd of Unicorns trotting gracefully along the beach toward the two angels. Most of them were white, with tiny babies among them. There was one black male among them.

"How did you know they were there?" Amy asked.

"I could feel their footsteps."

"I want to learn how to do that," Amy sighed longingly.

Azrael tilted his head. "Would you like to ride one?"

"Yes! I mean, could I?"

Azrael grinned at her eagerness. This was one of the things he loved most about her. She was full of life, and simple things made her happy, just as they did him.

As the herd moved past them, he held his hand to Amy. The black male trotted over to them, and Azrael stroked its mane tenderly. He softly whispered Angelic to the exquisite animal. Black unicorns were the rarest of any color. The unicorn was much more muscular than the rest of the herd and had scars on parts of its body. It had the same beauty that a rugged warrior would have. It rubbed its nose into Azrael's chest, and he laughed, then lifted Amy onto the animal's back. Azrael hopped in front of her. "Hold on to me, and you will be fine."

Amy wrapped her arms around Azrael's waist. "I won't fall?"

He placed his hand on hers. "Do not be afraid. I am here for you."

Azrael dug in his heels, and the unicorn cantered across the shore to catch up to the herd. Its hooves kicked up sand as it glided across the beach.

He kept his hand on Amy's as they rode. His gentle touch was all she needed to feel safe. She wished she could stay like this forever, her arms around Azrael. No one could make her feel as he did. Amy laughed with joy, and Azrael joined her laughter.

"I want to see more, Azrael," Amy implored. "Show me more of this world."

Azrael led the unicorn away from the herd toward a nearby forest. He dismounted and spoke words of gratitude in Angelic to the animal.

Amy reached out to pat the unicorn and intentionally fell off into Azrael's arms, grinning with an irresistible charm. "Sorry, I lost my balance."

"I know you have ridden before," Azrael informed her. He gazed into her eyes and smiled, and she realized he knew she had done it on purpose.

"I just wanted to make you smile and it worked."

She leaned in to kiss him. He was tempted and nearly met her lips with his own but moved away at the last moment.

"You know we cannot," Azrael said gently, setting her on the ground. "It is forbidden. No two angels may kiss, as it could lead to the creation of an angel, and only God may create angels."

Looking away, Amy murmured, "I know. I'm sorry. I don't understand why."

"We have talked about this many times. It is the law."

Amy's innocent eyes filled with tears. Azrael cupped her chin and tilted her head up to his gaze.

"What can I do to stop your tears from falling?" he asked.

Amy was slightly relaxed at his soothing tone. "Pick me up?"

He carefully lifted her into his arms. She embraced him tightly, closing her eyes and slowly allowing a smile to transform her face. He unfolded his broad white wings and wrapped them around her. Their love for one another shone around them, but such love could never be fully realized. Their love was a spark, brighter and warmer than any fire, but it could never be lit. The cold laws they abided by would always dampen it. They walked with their arms around each other into the forest with the black unicorn at their side.

Chapter 7

In the realm of Aeirliel, a vast army of angels covered the canyon of Gethyn. The brown gorge was devoid of life; its only distinguishing feature was endless dirt and sand. The air was filled with thick gray smoke and leaden clouds in the sky. Angelic archers stood ready with arrows notched in their bows along the hills and sides of the canyon. Each wore a pair of quivers on his back, which made an X on his chest. The quivers on their back could be adjusted to lay on their sides, making it easier and faster to draw arrows. They were only on their backs when they traveled. The archers wore smooth, light chest plates that appeared heavy and fit each one so cleanly that they felt like a second skin. The angels had helmets that covered their heads without compromising their vision. Like the chest plates, the helmets were very light, smooth and perfect in design. The angels each decided which additional armor pieces to add and in what areas based on personal preference. Within the ranks of the archers were high-ranking spell-casting angels. Most of these wore no armor because it would hinder their movements.

Within the canyon were angels armed with shields and a choice of weapons, ranging from a sword or spear to a staff or a two-handed ax. Most of the angels with weapons were heavily armored from head to toe. The armor differed in color to establish ranks, though most were shimmering silver. This armor was a work of art, just different from what the archers wore. Though the design varied, it was just as smooth and comfortable as it hugged the angels' bodies. Their keen eyes peered ahead of them and to the eerie clouds above. In the air, many angels were armed with spears, bows and various melee weapons. Their goal is to lure the beasts into the trench of death with the angels stacked all along the tall canyon walls.

Massive shadows emerged from the smoke-filled sky and flew down toward the ground. The Angelic army readied itself as hordes of dragons burst out of the smoke, belching fire. The angels on the front lines used their shields to block the fire; others used their magic to generate additional shields of green energy. The fire sparked on the finely crafted shields, and the angels threw spears at the passing dragons. Their weapons bounced off the iron hides of the larger dragons. When the spears made contact, the bigger dragons were unaffected, though some smaller dragons were smashed limply into the ground. The angels' attack barely dented the dragons' number as more dove out of the sky to flank the angels. Most of the angels in the valley were caught off guard. Many were engulfed in acid, fire and ice from the breath weapons of the dragons.

On the mountainsides, the archers unleashed volleys of arrows. Their arrows did little of their intended effect as only a handful of dragons tumbled to the surface. Most destroyed the arrows, using their breath to obliterate them before they landed. The magic-wielding angels fired off spells capable of crippling even the most mammoth dragons. A lightning bolt slashed through the sky and cracked into one beast. It crashed to the ground but survived the fall and the lightning bolt. Rising to its feet, it smacked several hovering angels with its wing, sending them flying a hundred feet in the opposite direction. Groups of angels swarmed the dragon to combat it with their swords, hoping their sheer numbers would overpower it.

Hundreds of horse-sized dragons worked toward the archers on the cliff sides. From a distance, they breathed fire or jagged bolts of electricity. They attacked with teeth and claws, ripping their foes in half as they got closer. One brave angel fired two arrows simultaneously and blinded a dragon, stopping it from chomping on his comrade just as he was knocked backward off the cliff and spiraling toward the ground. The battle raged on with bloody casualties on both sides.

Many blue sphere portals opened in the sky a short distance from the battlefield. Lucifer, Beelzebub, and Raphael materialized with legions of reinforcements. The three brothers paused to view the sporadic flashes of light on the battlefield. They heard their comrades' cries of pain and the dragons' vicious roars. Even from hundreds of miles away, the great eyes of the angels allowed them to see the combatants' positions in detail.

As impressive as an angel's eyes were, so too were the eyes and ears of a dragon. It would not be long before the creatures would smell, hear, or see the angels that had recently joined the fight. Lucifer assessed the battlefield quickly and realized he had to make decisions that would immediately impact the battle.

"Raphael, take a few angels with you and protect our wounded. Beelzebub, take a legion of angels and reinforce our flanks on the mountainsides. I will help drive back the main force."

Raphael and Beelzebub nodded and flew off to their positions. Beelzebub led a legion of angels into the clouds above the battle that covered their movement. Raphael gathered a few high-ranking angels and teleported to a safe place on the ground to set up a position to take the wounded. Lucifer turned around and faced the angels that remained with him. All eyes focused on him.

Lucifer looked at those he was about to lead. Their faces were expectant. He knew they were waiting for his speech to inspire them in battle. But there was no time to waste; his brothers and sisters died. They must act quickly before the dragons become aware of them.

"Brothers and sisters, show no fear or hesitation. Together, we will prevail." He drew his sword and hoisted it in the air. "For the Kingdom of God!"

Tens of thousands of angels drew their weapons and raised them in the sky.

"Luc-i-fer! Luc-i-fer! Luc-i-fer!" they chanted and pumped their weapons.

He paused for a moment and listened to the chants of his name. He felt the sound pass through him like thunder. It strengthened his desire to protect and lead his younger siblings to victory.

When Lucifer flew toward the battlefield, angels followed him like a tidal wave in the sky. He burst through a cloud, and the sun's light came with him. A few dragons were alerted and flew to greet them. Lucifer distanced himself from the legion of angels so he would be the first to collide with the dragon army. The first of many dragons clashed with him. He tucked his wings around his body and fell, swooping under the dragon's lightning breath and driving his sword up through its head. He kicked the dragon off his blade and strategically slammed it into an oncoming dragon. They both collapsed onto the terrain. Lucifer swiftly swooped to the next dragon and pierced its neck. A dragon came up behind him; he turned and shot a blast of blue energy at it. The power ripped a hole through the dragon's chest.

After dividing up his force to select areas on the east and west banks of the mountains, Beelzebub led a small group in a flanking maneuver against the horse-sized dragons who were wreaking havoc with the remaining angels on the ground. He slyly moved behind rocks and used magic to make his whole body appear as part of the rock. While using his magic and the heat from the sun to mask himself, he cautiously approached the flank of the giant dragon force.

Two dragons turned their heads, sensing something unusual happening with the rocks. Dragons have the most incredible vision of any creature. Some can sense invisibility spells but cannot discern what is there. In addition, others can adjust their vision to sense heat or cold and thus see as well at night as during the day. The only thing a being could do to protect himself against them was to blend into the terrain because if magic was used, some dragons could see the energy emitted from the spell. The two dragons slowly approached the strange stone.

Beelzebub readied his short and long swords; he teleported between the two dragons and cut off both heads simultaneously. He teleported through the dragons' positions, stealthily killing one or two after each jump. He finally arrived at the main force of his enemies.

"Excuse me, but I believe I found some friends of yours." Beelzebub tossed two dragon heads on the ground in front of the horde of slavering beasts.

Beelzebub! rumbled one dragon in a deep scratchy voice into the mind of Beelzebub.

All dragons spoke telepathically, as did other magical beasts. But only those with keen minds, such as angels, could hear their words.

"Such a delightful voice. Perhaps my blades can give you some lessons to improve it, as I did with your friends," Beelzebub replied with charm.

The dragons swarmed toward him and Beelzebub teleported a hundred yards away. He quickly blinked in and out among them, causing dragons to smash into each other as they teleported or flew after him in pursuit. Beelzebub waited until the last second to shift positions, causing dragons to shoot fire or lighting at their comrades as they attempted to kill him. A few dragons caught up to Beelzebub and snapped at his head, but he sprung up and flipped in the air, narrowly avoiding their dripping, feral teeth with an easy, confident smile. As he landed, he crouched down, gesturing to the hundreds of dragons to attack. The confidence in his eyes intimidated this group of enemies enough to cause them to hesitate.

Beelzebub's angels burst through the clouds and smoke to fire an onslaught of arrows and magical spells toward the dragons. Behind him, angels rose from their concealed positions in the sand and popped out of rocks to launch blasts of magical energy. The entire force of small dragons was decimated in an instant with little retaliation. Beelzebub leaned against the side of a rock and wiped his blade clean with a cunning grin.

Though Beelzebub and his angels had taken out a legion, dragons continued to attack from the air and the ground. The angels did their best to avoid being dive-bombed by the dragons. They avoided being chopped by massive teeth or gashed by their claws. An unlucky few were crushed or bitten in half. On the ground, the dragons were just as deadly. They whipped their long tails and knocked rows of angels across the battlefield. A few dragons demonstrated magical prowess and launched destructive spells of blue and red energy. The red energy soared in the air and exploded into the ground. The blue energy separated into small pieces and rapidly fired at the angels.

On the surface of the canyon, Raphael and a group of his assistants tried to pull some of their fallen comrades away from the heat of battle. Raphael saw a colossal dragon crushing an injured angel under its foot, but he hurled his spear and pierced the beast in the eye. He picked up the angel and quickly flew to safety.

In the air, Lucifer fought the battle completely alone and unaided. The dragons came at him from every side, but he fended them off. A few managed to land glancing blows. They cut his side and clawed his back, but he didn't flinch, and the wounds healed instantly. He dodged each attack easily. He suddenly stopped swerving and hovered in the air, delivering blows with his sword and fists. In a series of graceful moves that looked like a choreographed water dance in the air, he knocked dragons miles away from his position with a single blow. He cut his blade into their hides and blasted them with magical energy. Among the attackers, Lucifer appeared to have no equal, but an enormous dragon hovered just a few hundred feet away. The remaining dragons stopped upon seeing that their dragon captain had arrived.

The ancient shön dragon, Draaheson, stared down at Lucifer with wraithlike gray eyes. As with the angels, the older a dragon is, the more powerful it becomes. Draaheson's power had been compared to that of the dragon Queen, Verinity. Even Lucifer warily kept his distance as they glared at one another. Draaheson's glossy hide glistened in the light, and his black wings extended so wide that they eclipsed the battlefield. His body was perfect in size and form for an ancient dragon.

Lucifer and Draaheson fearlessly charged. Lucifer wove up and around the ancient dragon's strikes, trying to land a blow, but Draaheson smacked him down. Lucifer managed to recover before he hit the ground. He flipped in midair and landed on his feet. Draaheson towered over the mighty angel leader.

Lucifer, you cannot expect to defeat us. No matter the size of your army, we will overcome you, Draaheson stated.

"Our forces have you outnumbered beyond what you can handle," Lucifer replied, unphased. "Even now, we have flanked some of your positions. Look for yourself."

Draaheson carefully looked out into the distance. He saw his dragons slaughtered on the cliffs to his left and peered to his right to see the same. He saw Beelzebub standing with one foot on a rock; he blew Draaheson a kiss and waved.

The day is yours, Draaheson conceded. *But this war will be ours, I can assure you.*

"And I assure you, as long as I draw breath, you will never pass through the gates of the Heavens," Lucifer vowed.

Draaheson laughed. *We shall see courageous Lucifer of the Heavenly Seven. We shall see.*

Draaheson roared, and it echoed throughout the land. The dragons retreated from the battle. This day belonged to the angels.

Lucifer and his soldiers landed beside Raphael and the other healing angels. Raphael was in the process of closing one warrior's wounds as Beelzebub materialized beside Lucifer.

"The dragons have retreated on both flanks. I am having the wounded brought here," Beelzebub reported.

"Bring any of them in critical condition here to be cared for by Raphael. Make sure we leave a brigade to protect the healers and remaining wounded. Beelzebub, contact Michael, Uriel, Gabriel, and Zachriel for a meeting in the council room. I shall wait for you all there," Lucifer instructed.

"I will beat you there," Beelzebub assured.

"You never arrive at meetings on time," Lucifer reminded him.

"Maybe this will be a first," he suggested as he disappeared into thin air.

Lucifer looked at the battlefield to see the dead and dying. Angels were carrying their wounded comrades in for treatment because they could not walk. He hated to see so many casualties. One of the soldiers raised his sword to kill a wounded ancient shön dragon, Rnisen, but Lucifer teleported to the spot, blocking the strike with his sword. "Enough has died today. Get one of our healers to tend to this dragon."

"Yes, Lucifer."

The angel scurried off. Lucifer watched the last of the sun's rays retreating across the ground. The battle was over, but was it theirs, as Draaheson had said? With so much death, does anyone truly win a war? Lucifer knew the winner would be when both sides agreed to peace.

Chapter 8

In the council room of the Heavenly Seven, Lucifer, Michael, Gabriel, Zachriel, and Uriel sat in their chairs. They conferred about their recent quests for Mother Earth's soil.

"Perhaps we should try a different tactic than last time. Maybe more than just the three of us?" suggested Gabriel.

"I agree. We could easily take the soil with more angels there," Uriel said.

"Yes, but with more angels, Mother Earth may also unleash a larger force against us. I don't think we have the angels to fight a two-front war," Michael countered.

"I know everyone wants to get the soil as Father requested, but we must do it properly. I also know you all felt Mother Earth did not plan on giving you the soil, and you may be right. We must make another attempt to pass the trials." Lucifer added.

"Then what would you suggest? We go back and try again?" Uriel asked.

"No, not us. Let us send our pupil, Azrael. Father said that only one is destined to pass all three trials. Perhaps he is the one," Michael suggested.

"Azrael?" Gabriel was surprised. "Do you think it should be Lucifer or perhaps Beelzebub?"

"No, Azrael," Beelzebub replied as he entered the room late.

"I agree with Gabriel. I do not think Azrael is meant for this. If we send him, we should have an army ready when he fails to get the soil," Zachriel insisted.

"*When*? Do you have so little faith in him?" Beelzebub asked.

"Very well, *if* he fails to get the soil." Zachriel shrugged.

"Having an army supporting Azrael may be a wise plan, as I do not know that Mother Earth will part so easily with her soil, even if he does pass the test," Michael added.

All eyes turned to Lucifer.

Lucifer paused for a moment. "Very well, we will prepare for the worst if Azrael does not get the soil."

Changing the subject, Lucifer asked, "Have we tried to negotiate with the Queen of the dragons and the Matriarch of the griffins?"

"No, but I would suggest sending Beelzebub to the Queen. And perhaps Raphael could be sent to the griffins," Michael proposed.

"Raphael has healed most of our forces and should be available to negotiate with the Matriarch. With our army mended, we should be able to push the dragons back into their lands," Gabriel optimistically suggested.

"We must do more than that," Lucifer insisted, smashing his fist into his other hand with his words. "They wish to take over the Heavens and overthrow Father."

Gabriel looked thoughtful. "What if Raphael succeeds in his negotiations with the griffins? We will not have to worry about them. It should give us the force we need to send against the dragons and a force for the Earth."

"Then we may have an ally against the dragons," Michael added.

Raising an eyebrow, Gabriel shook his head. "I do not know if I would go that far, but having one less enemy would improve the war and bring the dragons to the peace table."

"Let us conclude this meeting," Lucifer proclaimed. "Gabriel and Zachriel, please relieve Raphael of his healing duties and tell him he must go to the Matriarch of the griffins wearing the red cloth of truce to negotiate peace. Summon Sariel if there are still many wounded. Beelzebub, you shall speak to the Queen of the dragons, wearing the same cloth. Michael, please update the Council of Nine on the progress of the war and the quest for the soil. We shall speak to Azrael about the quest for the soil during our next training session with him. That will be all, my brothers. Be well."

The Council of Nine was made up of members from each of the nine choirs of angels. They were a voice for each choir. They did not oversee the Seven but functioned as another body of leadership for each of the choirs.

****

A waterfall flooded into a clear pool of water. Around the pool was an oasis of trees heavy with ripe fruit. The unicorn drank at the edge of a pool. Azrael guided a blindfolded Amy to the water. They stopped, and Azrael removed the blindfold.

"Open your eyes," he whispered.

She opened her eyes, squinting momentarily at the light. Her face brightened with delight at the sight of the waterfall and the translucent pool of water. She raised her hands toward the fruit-laden trees, ripe with yellow, purple, and deep red. Their fragrance drifted over her, so enticing she could almost taste the fruit on the tip of her tongue. The air was moist from the splashing of the falls, which ran like liquid crystal into the shimmering pool below.

"Azrael, this is beautiful." She turned to him, but he was gone.

"Azrael. Azrael!"

He appeared behind her in an instant and touched her shoulder. Startled, she spun around. Amy sighed with relief and hugged him.

"Please don't tease me. I was becoming frightened."

"I promise, I will not leave you like that again. I wanted to give you a surprise."

He handed her a bouquet of white roses. She smiled, closed her eyes, and gently inhaled the fragrance of the flowers. Azrael unfolded a dark purple blanket for them to sit on.

An invisible wave passed through his soul. He felt the presence of someone very formidable, but he needed to find out who the entity was. He glanced around but could see nothing. All angels projected a presence, and each was unique. Its strength depended on its power. This presence felt familiar; he knew he had felt it many times before, but couldn't remember where. The presence seemed to fade in and out, and he could not pinpoint where or who the being was. But he was confident he felt something. Azrael shook his head and returned his attention to Amy.

"They're beautiful. But you gave me one for my naming day, and then you gave me so many other…."

"Must all gifts be for a reason?" he interrupted.

He offered her a seat on the blanket. The two of them sat together and observed the waterfall.

"No," Amy agreed. "Thank you. Can I ask you something? Why have you been placed here to teach young angels?"

"I have asked myself that question many times. I am not sure. The Seven have told me it relates to my destiny," Azrael said.

"The Heavenly Seven or the Seven Princes of the Heavens were the first of us to be created and highest ranked of the angels, but what about you? What is your rank?" Amy asked, her curiosity not dampened.

"Like you, I am a Seraphim, a high rank in the angelic order, but I am not in a position of authority. I am not as high as the Seven. Some regard me as a friend and others as their student."

"I am sorry if I am asking too many questions. Opal Eye gets grumpy when I ask too many questions."

"Then it is a good thing I am not him. Ask whatever you like," Azrael encouraged her.

Amy brushed her black hair from her face and leaned on her elbows, resting her face in her palms. Her dark eyes glowed with curiosity. "How are you able to do some of the things you do? Disappearing so fast and everything."

"Each of the magical creatures absorbs invisible particles called *maeraz*. It flows throughout the universe. Some angels absorb more than others, and the amount increases with age. It's the source of our magic and how I do the things I do."

"I must have fallen asleep for that lesson."

Azrael laughed. "A being such as Beelzebub absorbs anywhere from one billion to one hundred billion maeraz a day. Each spell costs a certain amount of maeraz. We can only do so many before we are depleted. This can tax our body and spirit should we do many powerful spells that demand countless maeraz."

She wrinkled her forehead. "Is that why you make swords?"

"Yes, but I am only one of many blacksmiths in the Heavens."

"But you are the best, they say." She could not hide the wonder on her face.

"I do not know that I am the best. Besides, I do not like fighting. I would rather not make swords."

"Will you show me some other things you can do with magic?" Amy asked in excitement.

"Of course. You only have to ask."

He stood up, offering his hand to lift Amy to her feet. They walked to the pool of water.

"Azrael, the water will eat me. I can't go out there."

He knew Amy could not swim, but it never bothered him. Azrael was a strong swimmer. Though he had planned to teach her when he had time, he was confident in his ability to keep her safe. He placed his hand on hers and gazed into her eyes. His azure eyes enchanted her.

"Do not be afraid," his voice calm and steady. "I am here for you."

His confident words and calm face gave Amy more strength and courage than anything else. Azrael gave her safety; he gave her happiness, but most of all, he gave her love. He could ask her to walk into a dragon's fire, and as long as he told her not to be afraid and that he was there for her, she would do it.

Azrael stepped into the pond. As his foot touched the water, it parted, allowing him to touch the ground instead of the water. With each step, the water parted around him, and he made a small path for Amy to walk on. Though he walked deeper, the water remained ankle high. Azrael made a three feet wide path with walls of water on each side.

Amy walked out to him, and they moved to the center of the pool. The water crashed behind them, covering the path he had made, but it did not touch him or Amy. A force around them, shaped like a sphere, prevented any water from touching them. They had about five feet of space within the globe. Amy reached out and felt the water flowing around them.

"How are you doing that?" she asked.

"I will teach you when we are together again," he assured her.

Above them, the sun gleamed down on them from the clear blue sky. As Amy slid her hand along the water, a white rose mystically appeared between her fingers. She turned to Azrael, and they smiled at one another.

"Stand on my feet, Amy," Azrael invited softly.

She carefully placed her bare feet on his. Azrael chanted a spell, and they lifted into the air. He encompassed them in water, and it flowed around them like a fountain. As they held one another, rising higher, Azrael's extended his wings to encircle Amy. Amy's innocent and joyful smile faltered momentarily as she looked at Azrael's face. They leaned into each other, embraced, and their lips lightly touched. Suddenly, they were locked in a passionate kiss they had so desperately desired. They had dreamed of and craved it; finally, it became a reality. Feeling the love the other felt was beyond anything they had imagined. No two beings in existence had ever shared as much love as this single kiss between Azrael and Amy.

Chapter 9

The Badlands of Aeirliel was a barren wasteland. Aside from a few hardy cacti and brush, the desert terrain was nearly lifeless. Here in the Southern continent, the dragons dwelled in great numbers. When they were first created, they were so numerous that they dominated the entire landmass of Aeirliel, but as the wars raged over the millenniums, their numbers diminished. They fought not only against the angels, but also against the griffins as they vied for possession of the land. At the moment, however, the griffins and dragons had a shaky truce. They were aligned against the angels with the common goal of getting a piece of the Heavens.

The cunning Beelzebub flew over the seemingly endless desert toward the immense mountain he knew the dragons used as an outpost. He sported a white cloth on his right shoulder to show that he came in peace. Beelzebub wore a flowing black tunic with a sleek white sleeveless shirt under another black-sleeved shirt; the clothes highlighted his pale skin and long, straight black hair. Despite the heat the colors attracted, he did not break a sweat. From a great distance, he saw two dragons standing sentry from their almost concealed location in front of the mountain. Although he had expended some *maeraz*, he still had plenty of energy, but he wanted to be conservative in the amount of magic he used entering the dragon territory. He teleported close to the mountain and landed on the ground. The spell of teleportation was not easily mastered. However, for Beelzebub, it was as easy as breathing. He folded in his black wings and held out the red scarf.

The dragons emerged from where they were waiting, immediately on the attack. But Beelzebub, as agile as he was cunning, quickly sidestepped the first dragon and sprang off its back to avoid the strike from the second. He flipped in the air, drawing one of his blades simultaneously.

"I am not here for a fight." He waved the white cloth at them. "If I were, do you think I would come alone? I come only to speak with Verinity."

They eyed him with mistrust and then finally nodded. *Follow us.*

The first dragon waved his claw over the mountain wall to unveil the magically concealed tunnel entrance. They led Beelzebub into the tunnel.

The cave was dimly lit with floating flames. As they followed the passageway deeper into the cave, the walls appeared smooth, crafted instead of naturally made from the Earth. They entered a vast cavern, which was stunning to the eyes. Thousands of tiny lights clearly outlined rich gray, black, and white stones that shimmered in the radiance. In the center of the room sat a fountain from which a small underground stream trickled.

The dragons disappeared, and Beelzebub moved toward Verinity, the dragon queen, who sat at an intricate table sipping tea. She blew steam out from her nose to heat it. To meet with him, she had become a tall humanoid female with long black hair that fell to her calves. She wore a skin-tight black and purple dress that exposed her cleavage. Sporadically her eyes changed from reptilian to humanoid.

"Welcome, Beelzebub. It is always a pleasure to see you," she greeted him with her mouth moving and the appearance that sound was generating from her lips.

He frowned. "Must you take this form? Can you not appear as all dragons do?"

"Does it unnerve you?" Verinity asked with a laugh.

"Slightly," Beelzebub admitted.

"Good." Smiling to herself, she indicated the chair across from her. "Sit and have tea with me."

Beelzebub sat carefully, noticing the dragons concealed all along the walls.

Verinity poured him some tea. "What brings one of Heaven's highest-ranking angels to my humble dwelling?"

"I come to seek peace with you and end this war."

"We have done this many times before, Beelzebub, but we always break our truce and fight again," she sighed. "We are called the soulless ones and are told that we do not have a place in the Heavens. It is why we continue to fight. We have a right to be there too."

"I am unable to offer you and the dragon society such a thing," Beelzebub said. "You would not be satisfied with the Heavens alone just as you were not satisfied by dominating Aeirliel. At one point, you did possess the entire realm and still quested for more. I only wish to bring peace between the angels and dragons."

"Because you are losing the war. But we will not stop our quest. Especially since we are so close to winning."

The angel did not flinch. "Please understand, it is not about winning; it is about bloodshed. Both sides have lost too many. Besides, I am tired of the fighting. I could use a break," he joked, knowing his request fell on deaf ears.

"Your fatigue is our strength. I am done speaking with you about this. We will crush the Angelic and take what is rightfully ours!" Verinity's shadow grew over Beelzebub, taking the shape of her dragon form though the humanoid figure before him did not change. The lights dimmed violently.

"Very well. I am sorry to have troubled you, your grace. I shall take my leave," Beelzebub bowed to her and teleported out of the cave.

Chapter 10

Azrael and Amy lay on the purple blanket, holding each other. Azrael stroked his fingers up and down her back. They were both happier than they ever had been.

"I liked kissing you, Azrael," Amy admitted shyly. "It was the most wonderful feeling."

"I liked kissing you, but we cannot do it again."

"Because of the law." Amy frowned.

"We could both be cast out of the Heavens or even killed. Just for that one kiss. I am not sure how the Seven will react to this."

"I am sorry." And she was—mostly. She held tightly to Azrael, unwilling to let go. Just when she thought they could indeed be together, just when true happiness had found a way into her heart, it seemed she was losing it.

"Do not be afraid. I am here for you. I will not let them harm you."

"It's not me I'm worried about. It's you I care for. What about God? What will He do to us?" Amy asked.

"I do not know. But whatever the punishment He has in mind, I will accept it. I will have to leave soon. I must continue my instruction with the Seven."

"Is Opal Eye still your teacher?"

"Opal Eye was selected as my mentor when I was first created. He taught me a great deal before the Seven began instructing me. His main purpose is to be the record keeper of Aeirliel. But since he is fluent in Earthly and Heavenly magic, he is an exceptional teacher in the magics. As long as you stay awake and pay attention," he added with a smile.

Amy blushed.

"Now I must truly go or I will be late. And the last thing I want is a lecture from Gabriel."

Azrael stood and helped Amy to her feet. She held his hands as tightly as she could but could not bear to look into his face. The pain of seeing his kind blue eyes would be too much for her heart to stand. "Will I see you again?"

He curled a finger under her chin and tilted her face up. She kept her brown eyes shut.

"Yes, you will. If only for one more time."

"Promise?"

"I promise."

She opened her eyes and took in his bright eyes and warm smile. Her eyes filled with tears as she embraced him. They held each other for a moment in the soft breeze. The wind gusted, and Azrael disappeared, leaving yet another white rose in her smooth hand and the hope of his return to her.

Chapter 11

In the southern courtyard of the Palace of the Seven, there was a garden filled with rows of every type of flower, arranged by species and then color. There were flowers the size of a watermelon and others as small as a snail. Though some exotic plants gave off heady fragrances or reflected light when it touched them, Michael wandered through the rose garden. He stared intently at the heart of a blue rose when Azrael appeared behind him.

"I personally like white," Azrael remarked.

"And does Amy like white as well?" Michael responded.

"You saw," Azrael stated.

"Yes, I did. Through Gabriel's orb, we see and record many things. But we make sure to always keep an eye on you. Father will want to speak to you about it."

"What do you think will happen to us?" Azrael asked uneasily.

"I am not sure. Do you think he will feed you both to sea serpents?" Michael said seriously.

"Michael!" Azrael cried.

"I jest. I am sure everything will be fine. You are one of his favorites, you know."

"Favorite or not, you still broke a sacred law," Gabriel stated as he appeared with the other five.

"Relax, Gabriel. You are too slavish about the law. One day it will backfire on you. It is not for us to decide Azrael's fate. Our little brother is only following his heart, just as Amy is," Lucifer intervened.

Lucifer undeniably was Azrael's big brother, and they shared a close bond. The two even resembled one another. While Lucifer was taller with a larger frame, their skin tone and similar facial features made them appear more like brothers than any other two angels. There was nothing Lucifer would not do for Azrael, and he protected him to a greater degree than any of his other younger siblings. Lucifer would always be one of the first Azrael would go to when he was troubled or needed advice. There was nothing Azrael would not do for Lucifer.

"Gabriel is right. What will others think now that one has broken the law?" Zachriel asked.

"I am sure our Father has something in mind already. Let us focus on Azrael's training," Lucifer said.

"I have a few lessons planned for today, and I believe Raphael wanted to review some of his healing methods too," Gabriel stated.

"We will do things a little differently today. Gabriel, you are on a time-out," Lucifer winked at Azrael, and they both smiled.

"You can stand in the corner just past the gardens and to the left," Raphael added.

"Shut up, Raphael. Lucifer, if you studied magic a little more, you could be teaching Azrael the skills he needs instead of me," Gabriel ranted.

"I have little time to study and practice," Lucifer explained indulgently. "I must be there for all my brothers and sisters."

"Little time to learn the sword too? Perhaps if you practice more, you might be able to rival Uriel or me as the best swordsman," Beelzebub interjected.

"It is true. If I had all the skills that each of you possesses, I would be a far better leader," Lucifer admitted with humility.

Michael placed his hand on Lucifer's shoulder.

"You are already the best leader we could ask for, regardless of skill with a blade or knowledge of magic."

"Thank you, Michael. How about a race, little brother?" Lucifer suggested to Azrael. "To the town center and back?"

"Last one back has to listen to one of Gabriel's boring lectures?" Azrael joked.

Lucifer and the other angels, except Gabriel, laughed.

"You're on!" Lucifer agreed.

They both took to the air and flew through the city.

"My lectures are not boring!" shouted Gabriel.

"No, of course not. They make Azrael fall asleep," Raphael continued teasing.

"I don't have to listen to this!" Gabriel protested.

"No one is keeping you here," Beelzebub pointed out.

Gabriel stormed away from the group of snickering angels.

****

Lucifer and Azrael glided across the city. They swooped under bridges and curved around buildings. Azrael stayed about five feet ahead. The town was quiet, with very few angels out walking or flying. Lucifer arced in his wings and shot down past Azrael with blazing speed. As they flew around the massive fountain in the middle of the city, Azrael flapped his wings rapidly to catch up. The two angels began to move so fast that they looked like shooting stars from a distance. Azrael hugged the walls as he caught up to Lucifer. He spun around an immense statue of Michael and blazed past his competitor. Azrael touched the ground a few seconds ahead of Lucifer.

As they landed, Lucifer and Azrael tucked their wings into their backs. Lucifer patted Azrael's right shoulder as the two rejoined the other members of the Seven.

"Looks like I must listen to Gabriel today, little brother. Why don't you learn a few new things from Beelzebub," Lucifer suggested.

"I would like that." Azrael agreed.

"Beelzebub, you are to teach him things, not just talk to him." Lucifer pointed at Beelzebub. "Promise me."

"You have my word." Beelzebub lowered his head.

Lucifer nudged Azrael. "Always be sure to get Beelzebub's word when it's important. No one is better at keeping it than he is."

"Thank you, Lucifer," Beelzebub said, then turned to Azrael. "Shall we?"

"Let's," Azrael replied, and they walked away.

Gabriel returned to the group of angels. "We should discuss our preparation for the possible battle for the Earthly soil," he insisted. "I also have reports that two of the Dragon Queen's eldest offspring were slain in battle. Let us send Beelzebub again to her once he is done with this lesson."

"I agree with you, Gabriel," Lucifer nodded. "Let's discuss this and other matters in more detail in the council room."

Chapter 12

Azrael and Beelzebub strolled around the perimeter of the palace courtyard.

Beelzebub walked with both hands behind his back. "Explain to me the difference between Earthly and Heavenly magic."

"The life force of the Earth and Aeirliel is used for Earth Magic. It can be best explained as a song, a forever-humming tune with notes and sounds. It is in everything, in the form of a soul, mortal, so there are mistakes within its make-up," Azrael recited.

"Very good. Which is why you could die if you should make a mistake in casting an Earthly spell," Beelzebub reminded him.

"Unlike Earthly Magic, Heavenly magic has none of these mistakes. But it is too perfect for some souls to hear and understand."

"Excellent. I know you prefer to use Earthly magic. Each soul is more adept at one form upon their creation."

"But between you and Gabriel, I've been learning from the best Heavenly and Earthly users in all the Heavens. Have you two ever done a magic duel?"

"No, but I doubt it would get anywhere. Since Heavenly is primarily for defense and Earthly for attack, we're essentially even, despite our age difference. Gabriel's magic is a pinch stronger than my own. He is older than me. Despite your age, I feel you will eventually be at our level."

"Do you truly think so? Sometimes I feel I am not strong enough or fast enough. I feel I do not know enough spells or the right tactic."

Beelzebub shook his head. "I believe you are destined for great things, Azrael. You may not have the right answer for everything at the exact moment, but you will solve the problem. Besides, look at me; I always find a solution despite the fact I might not use the method Gabriel would use or Michael."

"Yes, but you're Beelzebub."

"Yes, I am, aren't I," Beelzebub shrugged with a smile. With difficulty, he assumed a more businesslike expression. "What can you tell me about the angels and their ranks?"

"Lower-ranking angels function more as soldiers and messengers. There are more of these angels than the other triads. The middle ranks are designed to maintain the order set up by the high-ranking angels. The highest-ranking angels can function as either and give direction to the middle and lower-ranking angels. The high-ranking angels communicate directly with God much more frequently than the other triads."

The highest-ranking choirs are the Seraphim, Cherubim, and Thrones. They form the first triad of choirs. The next three are the Virtues, Powers, and Dominions. The last was Principalities, Archangels, and Angels.

"The higher the rank and greater the power, the more responsibilities one will have. This is part of why we have you train other angels," Beelzebub added.

Azrael paused, staring pensively at the endless cerulean sky. "I enjoy learning so much, Beelzebub. But I truly do not wish to use any of this training. I have fought in wars alongside you and the other Seven. I am tired of all the battles and wars. I do not want to fight in the war against dragons, griffins, or any other future war."

The older angel followed his gaze. "Nor do I. But we must all follow our destiny. We are training you because you have a great destiny to fulfill. But I don't think it involves fighting in this war."

"Good, I only want peace and happiness."

"And Amy?" Beelzebub asked.

Looking saddened, Azrael let out a long sigh.

"I want to be with her. I am happiest with her and feel the most at peace with her touch. I don't know if our Father will allow us..."

God appeared behind Azrael and alerted only Beelzebub to his presence.

"There is one way to find out; ask Him."

"Right now?"

"Yes, ask Me now," God said.

Frightened and amazed, Azrael knelt before Him. "Father, please forgive me. I did not mean to break Your law."

"Beelzebub, please excuse us," God requested.

Beelzebub bowed respectfully. Suddenly, Azrael and God were in a different place. It was an endless land of fields, ripe with bountiful crops, ready for harvest. There were also trees with purple, yellow, blue, and green fruits.

Azrael knelt in God's presence and stared at the ground. God gazed at his young angel. He loved Azrael and was always delighted to see and speak with him. He knew Azrael had a unique destiny, but He had also always known that this day would come.

"This is a serious law you have broken. I created it for many reasons," God informed him.

"I know. I am very sorry. We love each other, Father."

"I am aware," God said gently.

"What is our punishment? We shall accept anything you give us, but I have one request."

"Which is?"

Azrael looked up at his Father and stared honestly into His eyes.

"Please spare Amy's life. She is young and innocent about such things. She would not be in this situation if I did not encourage her. I take responsibility for it. Let me be the one held accountable for what happened."

Azrael lowered his head to the ground in humility. God stroked his white beard and smiled slightly. How amazing it was to hear this. He was truly touched and overjoyed. Azrael was even more than He had hoped him to be. This is why He had created him: not to be an angel who would follow his mind and the laws but also live by the dictates of his heart. That would always separate him from many of the other angels.

"Your compassion for Amy has touched me, Azrael. Neither of you shall die. I will allow a union between you and Amy. I will allow all other angels who feel as you both do, for a time, to have the same type of union. You love one another, and I will allow you to share that love and create. But there will come a time when the law will be renewed. Please rise, my Angelic son."

Azrael stood, relieved. "Thank You, Father. I am sorry for—"

God placed His hands on Azrael's shoulders. "You were forgiven before you asked, My son. Now I have a task for you. I had given this task to the Seven, but as I expected, they insisted upon doing it themselves. Several of them went and were unable to complete the task. They have realized and know it was you they should have sent." God explained what He required.

"How can I do this if some of the Seven could not?" Azrael wondered.

"You have had all the knowledge, strength, and heart of the Seven poured into you. You and you alone will obtain the soil."

"But wouldn't an angel with more experience be more suited for such an undertaking?"

"It is not always experience that makes a being the best choice for a task. Nor is it power or knowledge. Sometimes, it is the unseen potential within."

"Then why didn't You send me before the others?" Azrael asked.

"It must be understood that even the greatest of beings cannot do the deeds meant for another to do. Now everyone will know you alone were able to do this. That is part of your destiny."

Azrael was silent for a moment. His mind drifted to his future. He saw flashes of battles where opponents surrounded him in such vast numbers that they could not be counted. The vision was blurry, and he could not see their faces, as it was not a certain future, only a possible one. He saw creatures he had never seen before; their bodies appeared to be a mixture of wingless angel and bear. He slew anyone approaching him. But could not see an ally anywhere. The sight pained and saddened him. He did not want to be a man of war and hoped this possible future would not come to be.

"What troubles you?" God asked with concern.

Azrael described the vision of the future. "I do not want to be friendless and a killer of other beings."

"My son, please know that you are not a murderer. In the future, you may kill many, but it will not be killing from hate or malice. The deaths you may cause will be for justice and good. It is a distant and possible future you see. Obtaining the soil from Earth is only the first step toward one of many possible futures—toward your destiny. Do not underestimate Mother Earth or her trials."

"I do not want to disappoint You," Azrael said.

"You never have and never will. Just follow what the love in your heart tells you, as you always have done."

"I shall."

"Be well, My son. And though you cannot see Me, know that I am always with you."

"Thank You, Father. Be well."

A bright light expanded around God, and He disappeared. Azrael returned to the courtyard. While Azrael should have been happy, he could not help but be troubled. He had never been given such a distinguished task—something that none of the Seven could accomplish. He and many other beings in creation knew that the Heavenly Seven had gifts and abilities that surpassed all the other angels. Despite God's words of encouragement and praise, Azrael couldn't help but doubt himself. But the task had been given to him, and he would try to succeed with all his heart and soul. Beelzebub reappeared behind Azrael, who felt his presence and smiled.

"Did you have a nice chat?" Beelzebub inquired.

"I did. I have been tasked to obtain the soil from Mother Earth," Azrael informed him.

"Lovely, one less thing I will have to discuss with you," Beelzebub resonated with delight. "Shall we continue?"

Azrael nodded. He hoped his friend and brother could distract him for a time.

"How about a test of swordsmanship? I don't want to send you on your way without a little practice," Beelzebub suggested.

Beelzebub was much more than a teacher; he was Azrael's best friend. Their relationship was vastly different from any of the other Seven, as strong as the bond between Azrael and Lucifer. At one moment, Beelzebub would be Azrael's teacher, the next moment, his brother, and then he would become the young angel's pupil. Beelzebub never saw himself as greater or lesser than Azrael. He viewed and respected him as an equal. Their bond was so strong that death itself would struggle to keep them apart.

Beelzebub drew his smooth blade that curved at the tip, which Azrael had crafted. The runes were placed at the base of the blade. All crafted weapons had to have runes placed on them so the weapon knew what it was fighting for. Azrael pulled out one of his two curved swords. Beelzebub quickly lashed out in multiple fluid and rhythmic attacks. Azrael blocked or fluidly dodged each in the same pattern. Their fighting styles were very similar, but Azrael was the less physical and more precise of the two.

Beelzebub jabbed and swung his blade around. Azrael blocked the blows, spun, and countered with a whirling attack in midair. Beelzebub flipped over Azrael and drew his short sword as he landed on his feet. Beelzebub quickly attacked with both his swords. Azrael extracted another arched blade. The two cunning, agile, and stylized warriors continued to flip and spin around one another with perfect timing. Their fight appeared more like a dance; as one attacked, the other defended, and they switched roles. The tug-of-war war duel continued throughout the courtyard.

Beelzebub jumped in the air, and Azrael greeted him as they clashed and clanged swords. They struck at each other with great speed, flipping and whirling their blades around one another. While Azrael was supposedly the pupil and Beelzebub the master, an onlooker could not tell the difference, as both appeared to be masters of the sword. Beelzebub tried to sneak in a punch, but Azrael spun backward in the air. As he completed his spin, he extended his right leg, which connected with Beelzebub's chest. Beelzebub fell, flipping and spinning as he tumbled to the ground. He leaped to his feet with his blades whirling. While Azrael connected with a blow, it had little effect on Beelzebub's concentration. He made the fall seem almost intentional.

"Well done. I would say you are close to passing me and some of the other great swordsmen of the Heavens," Beelzebub said, signaling the end of the fight.

They lowered their weapons and spun them into their sheaths. Azrael descended to the ground. "Are you still holding back?" he asked.

"What do you think?"

"I can never tell what's going on with you."

"And I will always keep it that way," Beelzebub said with a confident grin.

Beelzebub knew that Azrael was the better fighter. He had known this from the very first day they trained. Azrael was naturally gifted beyond any angel he had ever encountered, but he had a vast amount of humility that Beelzebub admired and respected.

"Is there anything else we will do today?" Azrael inquired.

"Eager to speak to Amy?"

Azrael smiled. "Yes, very."

"I would have told you to go even if you had not asked," Beelzebub replied as he put his hand on Azrael's shoulder.

The two friends smiled at one another. There was no mistake; these two would always be lifelong friends.

Chapter 13

Amy slept before the waterfall on the dark purple blanket Azrael had left with her. She held the white roses loosely, even as she slept. A delicate breeze passed over her, disturbing her peaceful complexion; she lifted her head and awoke. "Azrael?"

She rose, curious.

Azrael appeared behind her. "Yes."

She spun around, smiling. "I missed you."

"And I you. I have wonderful news. We are allowed to be together as we have always wanted. I spoke with Father, and because of our love and for a time, He has abolished the law for all His angels."

Amy's face lit up with delight. "I can kiss you?"

"As often as you like."

She lifted her lips to his, and their smooth lips touched once more. She kissed Azrael's cheek and held him close.

"Thank You, Father," she whispered.

"I want to take you into the sky if you wish."

She pulled away. "I'd love to, but maybe I should finally awaken my wings."

"You are old enough to use them whenever you wish. But the first time they come out will be excruciating. It is usually very bloody. It is a good idea to be prepared and to have cloths around to help stop the bleeding. Of course, I will heal you too. It hurts the first few times, but eventually, it will be as easy as breathing. I was advised to do it quickly so it would not hurt as long."

As Azrael explained, he took her hands and led her through the tropical forest of thick green trees. Amy thought about what he had said as they found a calm stream trickling nearby. They held hands, and for a moment, they listened to the animals speak to each other.

"Will I be able to fly as you do?" she asked.

"Not at first. It takes time to learn how to fly."

She hesitated. "Maybe I should wait for another time."

"You always say that, but there never is another time," he smiled at her. She turned red and looked away.

"Perhaps after this time, we shall awaken your wings," Azrael suggested.

Azrael's white wings shot out of his back. Amy wrapped her arms around his neck.

"I'd like that," She beamed.

He took hold of her waist, and they ascended to the sky. Azrael flew Amy across the land and pointed out his favorite birds, animals, and the beauties of Earth's nature. A flock of winged horses glided past, and she squealed with excitement. Both angels laughed at her childlike wonder. Azrael turned his back to the ground and maneuvered Amy so that she was lying on his chest. He cast a spell that allowed them to float calmly in the air. She rested her head near his heart as they hovered above the clouds. They shut their eyes and absorbed this moment. Each reflected the other's feelings. Their hearts and breaths were steady and in synch. The day had come when they were finally free to be as they had always dreamed. This moment would be sealed within the memory of their souls to treasure forever.

"This is wonderful," Amy whispered.

Azrael slowly lowered them through the clouds, and they landed on the grass at the edge of the beach and walked on the beach.

"I must leave shortly and begin my quest. I have been assigned the task of collecting precious soil from the Earth," Azrael explained.

"I will be waiting for your return," She grasped his hand, and they continued to walk down the beach.

"So that I may answer more questions?" he asked.

71

"Yes, of course! I want to know everything. But I don't want you back for questions alone," she assured him by squeezing his hand.

"What would you wish to know?" Azrael asked.

"Anything that isn't boring. Something interesting that Opal Eye won't tell me."

He chewed his lip pensively and then nodded to himself. "There was a point when God allowed the first eight angels to explore their bodies so they could experience a childhood. They were allowed to be infants, and a group of animals raised each of them. Wolves raised Beelzebub, but he was too much trouble for them and had to be sent to the foxes."

"Did you get to be raised by animals too?"

"I did for a time before Opal Eye took me into his care," Azrael nodded. "The suliels raised me."

"Did you behave?" she teased and nudged him.

"Yes, I behaved."

"Suliels are the wolves that morph into griffins! See, I do not sleep all the time in my lessons."

"So it seems," he applauded her with a slight smile.

"What about Opal Eye? Why does he have an opal eye? Where did it come from?"

"As you know, his true Angelic name is Hapozetael. When I was young, I went through some of his things and saw a dagger. Hapozetael came in and saw me with it. He tried to take it from me, and I—"

"You stabbed him in the eye?!" Amy laughed uncomfortably.

"It was an accident. I did not mean to. But rest assured, he sees well regardless of that opal eye."

The ground suddenly began to shake, and Amy moved closer. "Why does the ground shake, Azrael?"

A dozen earth elementals shot up and surrounded them in a semi-circle. Azrael grabbed Amy and tried to fly away, but a wind slammed them violently into the ground. Azrael motioned with his hand, and a portal appeared for them to escape, but something slammed it shut. Azrael had never seen such a display of power. He did not know who could have caused it, but there was no time to ponder who had countered his spell. He drew both his curved swords.

"Stay behind me, Amy."

Azrael tried to stay as close to Amy as possible while defending her. He whipped his blades so fast they were a blur, slicing the first two earth elementals in half from their heads through their pelvises. As they crumbled, three more replaced each of them. Azrael spun, chopping off the arms and legs of three more. Amy was amazed at the remarkable speed with which he moved around her, protecting her from any harm. If any earth elementals came within five feet of her, Azrael quickly dispatched them. No matter how many there were, the earth elementals could not match his speed and quickness. Amy knew he would protect her. But an unexpected shadow eclipsed the sun. A dragon swooped down from the air and snatched Amy in its claw.

"Azrael!" Amy screamed in fright.

Azrael turned at the sound of her voice. Momentarily distracted, he was forced to leap into the air to avoid the strikes of two earth elementals. The creatures hit one another instead and crumbled. Azrael shot a burst of blue energy that smacked into the dragon. The beast dropped Amy; Azrael propelled his body underneath to catch her and landed softly on the ground. He quickly reacted to oncoming attacks, shifting Amy behind him as he spun ahead of her to block the blows. He defended her artfully through the constant flow of his blades. The dragon fired his acid breath at Azrael, but he rolled between groups of earth elementals. The earth elementals were engulfed in acid and melted into the ground. The dragon attempted to expel more acid, but a sword slashed into its neck. Lucifer appeared and punched the dragon on its nostrils. It crashed down into nearby trees.

"Little brother, you must flee with Amy before the Earth sends more enemies," Lucifer informed him.

Beelzebub appeared in the sky, soaring above Azrael. He shot a giant fireball that destroyed the remnants of the army of earth elementals approaching Azrael. Beelzebub touched down beside his friend amidst the smoking vegetation.

"Aren't I a welcome sight?" He grinned.

From the flames arose a fire elemental.

"Yes, I am filled with gratitude." Azrael thanked him with sarcasm.

"Oops. I am afraid I did not improve our situation," Beelzebub apologized.

Three more huge dragons appeared from out of nowhere. One scooped up Amy in its claws. Lucifer fought two of the dragons and prevented them from adding to the chaos.

"Azrael, help!" She called out.

Azrael took off from the ground, flying as fast as he could as he blitzed toward them. "Amy!"

Beelzebub focused his energies on the oncoming fire elementals. First, he covered his blades in a spell of cold. Then, he cast a spell that created a green energy shield that cut off fire elementals from reaching him. But more earth and fire elementals were made in front of the long and wide energy shield to attack Beelzebub. He teleported around the fire elementals and earth elementals, making quick work of them with his ice-covered blades. As he froze the fire elemental, they turned into ice elementals, as he had hoped. He fired a blast of red energy. The ice elementals shattered into millions of pieces.

Azrael charged toward the dragon that had Amy. The dragon shot a blast of blue energy, but before it could hit him,

Lucifer dashed to his aid after making quick work of the other two dragons. He knocked Azrael out of the way, and they crashed to the ground. Lucifer turned his body toward the ground to take the impact of the landing. They both got to their feet. Amy screamed as the dragon carried her away, flanked by two of his wounded companions. The fire elementals turned into smoke, and the earth elementals returned to the Earth. Azrael attempted to pursue the dragons. Lucifer stopped him with his hand.

"It would be better not to."

"Why do the dragons want with Amy?" Azrael asked.

"Why indeed?" Beelzebub added.

"I cannot leave her. I must go after them." Azrael was determined. He leaped in the air and flew after them.

Beelzebub and Lucifer followed, flying on either side of him.

"I know you love Amy, but you must complete your quest first. It is your duty and your destiny," Lucifer tried to explain.

"No, I must save her."

"You have a duty to perform. Would Amy want you to abandon that?" Beelzebub inquired.

"No, she would want me to complete it," Azrael admitted. "But that doesn't mean I should not save her."

"I do not believe she is in any immediate danger," Beelzebub observed. "If they were going to kill her, they would have done so."

Azrael stopped and hovered in the air. Lucifer and Beelzebub did the same.

Azrael knew his brother was right. But it was an injustice to his heart and soul. No sooner did he learn he was allowed to be with Amy, than she was taken from him. If she were to perish, his heart would be shattered.

"I will begin my quest, but no harm had better befall her."

"I will look into why the dragons have taken Amy and do what I can," Beelzebub promised.

"Thank you, Beelzebub. And thank you for saving me, Lucifer. I am in debt to you both."

"You owe me nothing. What are big brothers for?" Lucifer responded.

"I am a small being and have just been handed a large task that I do not know if I am up to the challenge," Azrael said.

"You are not so small. Only a finger's width smaller than Beelzebub." Lucifer showed with his finger.

"You know what I mean."

"I must go and prepare more angels. Meet me in the chamber of seeing. Perhaps we can find clues on Amy's whereabouts before you leave for your quest. Be well, little brother,"

"And you," Azrael replied.

Lucifer was engulfed in light and disappeared.

"I wish you were coming with me. I could use a good friend," Azrael commented to Beelzebub.

"Good friend? I am a great friend!" Beelzebub joked.

They both chuckled, and Beelzebub put his hand on Azrael's left shoulder. "This is something you must do on your own."

"I know."

"Stay focused on the task at hand. I will speak with you as soon as I know something about Amy. Be well, my brother."

"Be well."

Beelzebub wrapped his cloak around himself and disappeared within his cloak circularly.

Should he start now? Azrael wondered. First, he would speak to Lucifer. Then, he would get advice on the trials of Mother Earth. He did not know the trials or how to overcome them; he knew he must be cautious, prepared, and astute. And he knew exactly whom to speak with on such an important matter.

Chapter 14

Lucifer and Azrael entered the *chamber of seeing* together. At the center of the room was a white globe the size of a coconut held up by a stand made of white stone. The two stood on opposite sides of Gabriel's seeing orb.

"I will look in parts of Earth. You can search Aeirliel," Lucifer instructed his younger brother.

They peered deeply into the orb and quickly searched through the two worlds. They scanned through deserts, ice plains, jungles, and oceans for any sign of Amy. After a few minutes of searching, Azrael paused and looked at Lucifer's green eyes.

"I wish to ask you something," he finally said.

Lucifer stopped his search and looked up. "What is it, little brother?"

"I have been given this quest, but it is bigger than me. I feel many others are more capable of doing this. You are one of those beings."

Lucifer's gaze softened. "Azrael, over the numerous millenniums, much about you has changed. But the one thing that has lingered is your self-doubt. I am hoping that it will change to confidence and humility."

Lucifer walked around the orb to stand next to Azrael. He towered over his little brother.

"From the moment Father created you, I knew you would be special. God had stopped making angels in the masses to make you alone. I asked Him why, and He said it was because He wanted to feel what it was like to make only one angel for the last time. Right then, I knew you would be special."

"I did not know that I was made alone."

"You were the last to be made that way, as I was the first. After a time, God told us to pick you as a pupil, to help train you to become what you were meant to be and fulfill your great destiny."

"I think I still have a long way to go. There is much that I have to learn." Azrael let out a sigh and hung his head.

Lucifer put his hand on Azrael's shoulder, and he looked up. "We have fought together in countless wars, and I have helped you in your training. I even flew with you on your first flight when you awakened your wings. Azrael, do you remember when we fought the ancient dragon together? The most recent one, I should say."

"That's something I will never forget," he assured him. "It was part of what started this current war with the dragons."

Azrael thought back on his most recent confrontation with an ancient shön dragon. The fight lasted for hours, and it had been hard fought from the start to the end. If Lucifer had not come to help him, he would have died. But he was there the moment Azrael whispered his name for help. He did not realize they had set a trap for Lucifer. Azrael had felt guilty for calling out his name, but he did think he had redeemed himself for it.

"You were amazing. Your skill, magic, and wit could not be equaled that day. There is no one I would have preferred at my side that day aside from you. I am sure the Queen thought twice after that assassination attempt. She picked the wrong angel to use as bait."

"Yes, but you nearly died," Azrael said.

"But I didn't, and it was because of you."

"That day is different from what I must do now."

Lucifer wrinkled his brow. "Why is that?"

"Because you were with me."

Lucifer laughed. "And here I am, just the same. Erase any doubt you have of yourself. Do you think Amy doubts you?"

Azrael put his fingers to his chin and thought for a few moments. If there was anyone aside from his Father who did not question his destiny, it was she. Right then, Lucifer's words hit him. He could not doubt himself; Amy needed him.

"You are right, big brother."

"I will continue to search for Amy. I will look for as long as I can. Right now, I think you have other things to tend to."

"I plan to speak to Opal Eye before I begin my quest," Azrael informed him.

Lucifer raised his eyebrows. "A wise choice. I may not be there with you for the journey, little brother, but know that I am always there for you when possible."

"I know. Be well, Lucifer." Azrael touched Lucifer's shoulder as he walked to the door.

"As you, little brother."

Chapter 15

Gigas was made up of open terrain surrounding one of the enormous mountains in Aeirliel. Because of its configuration, the wind was constantly blowing to some degree. It extended from the coast, protected by small islands off the mainland, to a wall of mountains that isolated the area from the rest of Aeirliel. In Gigas lay the kingdom of the griffins. The landscape was perfect protection from any who would invade by land or sea.

While Beelzebub went to his meeting with the dragons, Raphael went to an assembly at the same time. He calmly walked with a spear in hand down a dirt path that led to the kingdom of the griffins. Like Beelzebub, he wore a red cloth on his shoulder and around the top of his spear. He heard a birdlike cry for help from a point not far off the path. He veered from his course to investigate the sound. As he got closer, he chose his steps carefully and shielded his body behind the landscape's numerous large rocks, leery of attack. Finally, he peered around a large mound of rocks and saw a baby griffin with a broken wing and foot. Raphael emerged from the rock's protection to show himself to the griffin. The young griffin was frightened at the sight of the angel.

"You won't get very far with neither of them working," Raphael observed.

Raphael spoke nonthreatening assurances in the griffin tongue telepathically as he approached the crippled chick. The baby griffin's fears calmed as Raphael moved slowly forward. He knelt at the baby's side and whispered a healing spell. White energy was released from his hands over the baby griffin's injured wing. As the light faded away, the griffin could move her wing. It clucked and murmured noises in its tongue.

Raphael laughed. "You are such a cute little thing."

A giant silhouette crept over him. He looked over his shoulder to see an adult griffin.

State your purpose, angel, or I will see to your end.

"My end? For what? Healing one of your young ones? As you can tell, I come here in peace," he motioned to the red cloths on his shoulder and spear. "I would hate to see your hospitality if I actually harmed her."

How do I know you didn't? The griffin challenged.

"That is a ridiculous notion. Do you know who I am? I am—"

The griffin lashed out at him. Raphael spun under the attack and pushed his halberd into his enemy's chest. The griffin shrieked in pain and shot out a line of lightning. Raphael rolled under the lightning while finding cover behind a rock. The griffin smashed the stones with its claws, and the angel was forced to leap before the rubble could cover him. Raphael chanted a spell and fired an energy pulse at the griffin, who tried to attack multiple times but was blocked by the invisible force from the spell Raphael had cast around it.

"Now we can be friends." The angel nodded with approval and returned his attention to the injured baby. He gently touched the other break, causing another bright white light to shine around her leg. It, too, was now healed. She leaped on Raphael, knocking him to the ground while she licked his face. He laughed and the baby griffin flew away. Raphael got to his feet and walked over to the adult griffin.

"Why can you not be more like your children? I am not here to create more bloodshed. I am here to end it. As you can see, I healed her wounds and shall do the same for you. After that, I request that you please take me to the Matriarch. Are we in agreement?"

The griffin nodded its proud head.

Chapter 16

Opal Eye sat in his study, writing on parchment. Scrolls hung down from the shelves; books were piled on his desk, and the floor and tiny lights danced throughout the room. A small candle glowed on his desk as he wrote angelic writing on the page. One of the little lights landed next to the candle. It was a fey named Morrigan. As with most of the fey, she was barely wearing anything—just a very short red cloth tied tightly around her waist and a crimson cloth over her top that exposed her belly and hugged her breasts. It appeared either could fall off and expose her with a simple touch. She bent over before the candle with her face and hands close to the flame.

"I am looking to warm myself by the only fire in this room," she commented. "Don't you think you could start a larger fire in the fireplace to give us a little more warmth?"

"I am sure you could use magic to do the same. I am comfortable right now," Opal Eye replied.

"If I wore as many robes as you, I would be warm too," Morrigan countered.

"Perhaps you should consider doing so. If you did, maybe your father would not have left you and your sisters here under my watch."

"Where would be the fun in that?!" she exclaimed.

Morrigan bent her bottom towards the fire and peered up at Opal Eye while batting her lashes. A wind blew through the room, making it appear she had put out the candle flame through her rear. Some of the scrolls on the desk moved, and Opal Eye raised an eyebrow at her.

"It wasn't me! I did not do that!" Morrigan protested.

"One day, I hope you will find a way of arriving without my knowing." Opal Eye returned to his writing.

Azrael phased into sight. "I did not want to be rude."

"Azrael, you are always welcome in my chambers," Opal Eye assured him. "What brings you here?"

Morrigan flew up to Azrael's face.

"Yes, what brings the handsome pupil of the Seven here?"

"Bah! Leave the man be. You know he has no interest in you, Morrigan."

"It doesn't mean I can't flirt." She smiled and leaned into the young angel.

"I am here for Opal Eye's council. I was hoping he had some components for spells," he responded.

"You are not here to see me?" Morrigan asked.

"I am sorry, but no. I must complete my quest and then do what I can to save Amy," Azrael apologized and walked around her to Opal Eye.

"Ohh, that's so romantic. Did you hear that, sisters? He plans on saving his love."

Morrigan's sisters made giggly sounds, batting their eyelashes and praising him for being such a hero.

"Confound it!" Opal Eye muttered. "Would you all be silent? I have not yet conferred with the man, and you all drool over a deed he has yet to accomplish."

The fey women became silent and made faces at Opal Eye behind his back. Opal Eye opened his cupboards that held vials and jars. He rummaged around and placed a select few on the table before Azrael.

"I believe I can help you with both counsel and components. You must face three trials to obtain Mother Earth's soil. The Trial of Life, the Trial of Balance, and the Trial of Death."

"And if I complete these, will she give me what I need?"

"The prophecy says she will give the Earth to the one whom she deems worthy of having it. The trials are meant to be her way of gauging if you are such a being. I see no reason why she wouldn't give it to you." He paused. "I know what happens in two of them. I know they occur differently for each who attempts them. The Trial of Life is to obtain the egg of a griffin from the top of a great mountain. But you must obtain the egg and get it to hatch."

Azrael was nonplussed. "And the other?"

"The Trial of Balance is to free the phoenix the mermaids have imprisoned. Water has flooded a portion of the Earth, and the balance will only be restored at the release of the phoenix."

Azrael absorbed all this. He paused and thought about how he would approach the two trials. He was concerned about the trial of death because Opal Eye knew nothing about it and he felt it was linked to his destiny. "Do you know anything of the Trial of Death?"

Opal Eye regarded him steadily. "Death is different for each being, Azrael, and so is the trial itself. I wish I could tell you more."

"You have told me plenty, my old friend."

Opal Eye packed vials and pouches of substance in a backpack.

"Avoid using any spell that contains an element of the Earth because it can be turned against you. Only spells of magical energy should be used for defense or attack. They are least likely to be countered by the Earth."

Azrael waved his hand over the backpack, and the bag shrank to a size small enough to fit in his hand. He put the backpack in a pouch on his belt and paused; his thoughts had returned to Amy. He wondered if this would be her fate if they were together: enemies seeking her out to hurt him. All he wanted was a peaceful life with her.

"What troubles you?" Opal Eye inquired.

"In following my destiny, will war and death always walk at my side?" Azrael asked.

"You know of peace and love, Azrael. And because you know of it, you will fight to have it. Be well, and may God be with you."

Chapter 17

Deep in the southern region of Aeirliel, Beelzebub sat within one of the dimly lit caves of the dragons. He was softly turning a wine glass in his hand. The dragon's blood wine was nearly black as it spun in his crystal glass. He had yet to reveal his knowledge of the Queen losing two of her eldest offspring. He sat comfortably and confidently in his chair, studying Verinity across from him.

Verinity, on the other hand, did not possess his calmness and certainty. Her eyes narrowed on him, and she folded her hands under her chin, fingertips touching her lips. She was in a humanoid form because she knew it annoyed Beelzebub.

"I am growing impatient with your endless meetings, Beelzebub. It's a wonder I have not killed you."

Her comments did not phase Beelzebub's composure. He took a sip from his wine glass. "If you kill me, you will not be able to hear my tragic news."

Steam spewed out of Verinity's nostrils, and her eyes briefly changed to those of a serpent.

"You underestimate the pleasure it might bring me to see one of the Heavenly Seven dead. Any loss I may have suffered will be only a small setback from our conquest."

"Even the death of your eldest son and daughter?" he said softly.

"You lie!" she protested. "None of the Angelic could slay them!"

"Verinity, I give you my word; they are dead. I am sorry for your loss." Though she had just threatened his life, Beelzebub felt compassion for her situation.

Verinity's face softened, and her eyes became glossed with tears. She knew Beelzebub never broke his word. "Then…it is true."

Clear blue tears streaked down her soft pale face. She let out a scream, and it became more of a roar. Dragons spewed into the room, crawling on the ceiling and along the walls. They moved quickly but tried to stay in the shadows. Others entered, completely cloaked with a spell of invisibility.

Beelzebub noticed the numerous dragons but did not panic, as many others would have. His escape had been carefully planned should any of them attempt to attack. Beelzebub was always careful to think through all outcomes and possibilities and be prepared for each. He was ready to use whatever means necessary, be it magic, the sword, his strength, or his wit. He carefully slid out several components for a spell hidden in his shirt sleeve while sipping his wine with his other hand. The dragons moved to attack, but the cave shook, and the fire dimmed to a soft blue color.

"I gave no order to attack the angel Beelzebub!" Verinity the Queen thundered the command speaking in her human voice.

My Queen, the Angelic must pay for the deaths of your children with the death of one of their most treasured Seven. As the dragon finished speaking, he leaped off the wall at Beelzebub.

"No!" she screamed.

Verinity fired a jagged purple bolt of lightning at the dragon. The lightning cut an enormous hole through the dragon. Before its corpse could crash onto Beelzebub, he teleported to a safe spot in the cave, calmly sipping the last drop of his wine as he reappeared.

The dragon's corpse caused the others to flee, but the Queen remained humanoid. Beelzebub leaned on the side of the cave and walked back over to Verinity.

"We have had many wars over the millennia. The dragon empire's losses have been as countless as the angels. The last time I lost one of my children, it angered me, and we launched a massive assault on the Seventh Heaven. It is different now. I feel more pain and sadness. Similar to when one of the firstborn dragons died. I know now why God wishes this to end. I will admit that part of me wants to continue this war to avenge them, but it will only cause more bloodshed," she finished with a whisper.

"What if we were to make a pact different than any previous one?" Beelzebub said.

"What do you suggest? We want to be a part of the kingdom of Heaven, yet we are denied it. We deserve a place there. We are far superior to any angel, and you know it," the Queen reminded him.

"What if you took seven of your ancient shön dragons and made them pledge an oath to fight with an angel to which they would be bonded? In turn, those seven would pledge to fight for the dragon. Those seven dragons would be given a place in the Heavens and would be a voice for the dragons. At the same time, seven angels would be given a voice among the dragons."

The Queen leaned on her fisted hand, considering. "I know of a few who can be trusted and whose loyalty to me will be as great towards the angels. But it will be difficult."

Beelzebub knew that dragons had a different mindset than other creatures. They needed to be raised by someone of a good heart to overcome their vicious and aggressive tendencies toward other creatures, as that was in their nature. The Queen and others were exceptions to that rule. But finding seven ancient shön dragons who fit the description would be difficult.

"I will find you seven dragons for the Heavenly Seven, and our two peoples will know peace," the Queen concluded.

"Thank you, Verinity. I will speak to the rest of Seven about this. While I cannot promise this will happen immediately, I hope we can eventually reach this agreement in full."

"I understand, and I will prove my alliance to the angels," Verinity said.

"Perhaps, you could start by helping me with a problem. What do you know of an angel named Amy?" Beelzebub asked.

"Nothing. Is she of importance to you?" Verinity responded.

"Not as much to me as she is to Azrael. She is his love. She was taken from him by a fire dragon."

"I know nothing of such a capture. I will look into it for you," Verinity promised. "Azrael, the pupil of the Seven?"

"Yes."

"I know Azrael. As soon as I learn anything, I will inform you immediately."

"You have my thanks."

"Please be sure to tell the Heavenly Father that the war between you and the Dragon Queen is over. However, I fear that not all will agree to cease attacks against the Angelic. But you have my word that I will try to maintain peace. Do I have yours?"

"You have my promise, your grace," Beelzebub bowed.

"It is settled. May peace between the angels and dragons begin."

Chapter 18

Azrael walked along the beach where he and Amy had ridden the black unicorn. He followed tracks of hooves to a small pool of water, similar to the one where he had taken Amy. He did not see the unicorn among the herd. As he turned to leave in defeat, the rare black alpha male stood before him.

"You must have known I was looking for you." Azrael smiled as he spoke in Angelic tongue. "My friend, I must ask you again for a ride."

The unicorn nickered as the angel gently stroked him. It welcomed his touch.

"The area I must go to is protected by magic. Otherwise, I would go there by other means. I could use a good friend, but I warn you, this will be far more dangerous than our last ride together. I would understand if you would rather not."

Again, it nuzzled him. Azrael mounted, and they stormed off down the beach. He whispered words of Angelic in its ear. The unicorn's horn glowed in response, and it galloped swiftly up the coast and down a path. It ran so fast that its hooves barely touched the ground. Azrael rode over many hills and through endless forests before reaching the Great Mountain of the Earth.

Azrael dismounted and strode next to the proud unicorn as they approached the Great Mountain. It was massive and rigid as it reached its summit in the sky. At the tip of the peak was the griffin egg. Clouds blown by fierce winds surrounded the crest and acted as protection from any unwelcome intruder.

Azrael peered up at the mountain, which dwarfed him.

"I am not strong enough to handle the winds."

The unicorn nuzzled him in encouragement. It then tried to lead the way up the mountain. Azrael stopped him from proceeding.

He spoke Angelic. "No, no, my friend. As much as I would love for you to join me, I must do it alone. Please return to your brothers and sisters. Thank you for carrying me this far."

The unicorn trotted back into the forest. Azrael unfolded his white wings and sprinted at the mountain. He flapped his wings and rose into the air. Instead of fighting against the wind, he tried to use it to aid him in getting to the peak of the Great Mountain. His wings accumulated ice as he glided higher, battling the winds, and he struggled not to fall. He pulled something from his pouch, and a red glow shone from his hand. The ice on his wings melted, and he pushed himself close to the summit.

Azrael tried to land but was blown away from the mountaintop. The winds focused directly on him like a large giant had taken a deep breath and blew the air out at him. He approached from another angle, but again the winds were too strong. He climbed above the wind current and dive-bombed to a space on the peak. As he moved swiftly toward the ground, he curled his legs in, somersaulted on impact, and sprang to his feet.

Immediately a boisterous wind slammed into him. Azrael crossed his arms over his face as he battled to walk forward to the griffin egg. The wind pushed him to the edge. He grabbed something from his pouch as one of his heels slid off the edge. He threw the compound into the ground, and a thick white cloud burst in front of him. The fierce wind blew brutally against him, and he lost his footing. The white cloud faded away, and Azrael was gone. The roaring wind blew on the mountain, but nothing else was seen or heard.

Suddenly, Azrael burst up from the ground next to the griffin egg. The spell he had used allowed him to travel underground, away from the wind. The egg was so big that he had to lift it with both hands.

"Now, how do I get you to hatch?"

A figure loomed behind him, and he saw the creature's shadow overtake him. He quickly sidestepped to avoid a fierce attack from an immense griffin.

How dare you steal my egg? The Matriarch of the Griffins bellowed.

"I was unaware the egg had an owner," Azrael admitted.

Foolish angel! You know that God made the griffin, and we make eggs. Of course, the egg has an owner! Ina, the original Matriarch of the Griffins, declared. She had been missing for several centuries. She had no surviving offspring, having lost all of her children in the wars.

Azrael was stunned at the sight of her as he recognized the griffin. "Well, yes. I did not know it had a living owner."

Ina had lost countless eggs to an assortment of attacks and misfortunes. After years of dealing with the pain of losing her young, she took this one egg away from her people to the safest place she could find on Earth. She had guarded it on the Great Mountain and had been ever-watchful for foes who might conquer the fiery winds that protected her egg. But Azrael knew none of this. She leaned in to strike at the angel.

Azrael ensured he had a tight grip on the egg and opened his wings. He was immediately lifted into the air by the winds. The Matriarch pursued him with great haste. He flew with the violent gusts, but they constantly adjusted to aid the griffin and blow against him.

Return my egg to me. I must protect it from creatures like you. Someone is always trying to hurt my young, Ina cried.

She swiped at him, and Azrael carefully evaded the strike with great poise.

"I am not here to take your egg. I am here to help the egg hatch."

You lie! Why would an angel come to the aid of the griffins?

She clawed at him many times. Azrael wove in, out, and around the blows. Ina shot a giant bolt of blue and white energy at him. He put up a green energy shield that blocked a portion of the blast and flew in a loop to avoid the rest.

"I am not here to fight you. I am not your enemy," Azrael yelled as he flew to the ground.

He landed at the mountain's base. Ina landed near enough to him to remain a threat. She stalked closer while digging claws and talons deep into the Earth. She lashed out at him again, and he used his keen agility to avoid her assault. Azrael sprang and darted around her blows, as a squirrel would avoid being captured by a bird of prey. He was swift, even for an angel. The chase lasted a few minutes, and her claws came inches from his back and stomach. Azrael took special care to protect the egg while dodging its enraged mother.

Struggling to maintain his balance, he held the egg in one hand and nearly fell. The griffin leaped in the air to seize the opportunity to cripple the nimble angel. As Azrael turned to face the oncoming air strike, the unicorn burst in front of him. The griffin extended her wings to slow and come to a stop. The black unicorn's horn glowed, and he stomped his hooves as he moved toward the Matriarch.

A unicorn coming to the aid of an angel, Ina said. *He acts as though you are one of his own.*"

"Please listen to me," Azrael pleaded. "Maybe I can help you."

Ina knew that angels had relationships with various animals with whom they could communicate telepathically. Still, it was rare for a unicorn to have such an intense bond that it would risk its life to save an angel. This angel was different. Unless it was an illusion; but the griffin saw no signs of magic around the unicorn.

Very well, angel. I shall listen to you. This unicorn has given you a chance to speak.

"You say the egg has not hatched in centuries. Have you been with the egg all that time?" he asked.

I have had little time for that, with all who come to take it from me, Ina accused.

"Perhaps that is the reason it has not hatched. It has not felt the warmth from its mother."

The Matriarch tilted her head. *You could be right.*

Azrael held out the egg. "Here, give warmth to your child."

She carefully grasped the egg, putting it close to her body and wrapping her wings around it. For a long time, silence fell as she bent her head over the egg. The winds ceased, and the chill receded as the hours crept by.

Azrael patiently waited. He knew such things did not happen in an instant. Eventually, he heard a tiny crack and then the sound of the egg breaking open.

The Matriarch unfolded her wings, and before her was the baby griffin. It looked up into the gentle eyes of her mother. Ina wept at the sight of a child she had longed to have for centuries. The mother let her child walk freely, and it saw Azrael. The baby griffin stumbled toward him, jumped into his arms, and nuzzled his chest. She leaped back to the ground and used her wings to slow her descent.

The newly made mother studied the unknown angel. She saw his genuine smile as he looked upon her child and realized he was what he claimed to be. She immediately knew that the war between her people and the angels must end forever. If one angel could offer such kindness to her, there must be others who would do the same.

I am Ina, Matriarch of the Griffins.

"You have been considered dead for centuries by certain people," Azrael informed her.

No, not dead. I left my people ages ago, heartbroken, but you have mended that with your compassion and sincerity. Angel, what is your name?

"I am called Azrael."

I apologize for my behavior, and thank you, Azrael. I assure you that every griffin will know of this day and the kindness of the angel Azrael.

"I am honored and humbled." He bowed his head.

Are you a Seraphim? She asked.

"Yes, I am."

Aren't you a little small for a Seraphim?

Azrael chuckled. "I have been told that."

Nevertheless, you have proven to me that even little beings possess incredible strength and courage. You may know very little of me, but I assure you, my people will know and speak your name with great praise. I am in your debt. Farewell, Azrael.

Ina picked up her newborn and flew away. Azrael was pleased with what he had accomplished. He let out a soft sigh and smiled. It was not an easy test. His heart was still pounding. A shimmering blue and white portal opened in front of him.

"You have passed the first of my trials, Azrael. Through this portal lies the path to the next, the Trial of Balance," Mother Earth told him in the voice of an adolescent girl.

Azrael turned to his friend, the unicorn, to show his gratitude. He stroked the side of his neck and petted its nose.

"My friend, you are one of the bravest beings I have met. Thank you again for your help. When this is over, I hope to make it up to you," he said in Angelic tongue.

The unicorn made various noises as though speaking. Azrael could understand what he was saying within his mind and laughed.

"I know you would, and you would be of great help too." He patted the animal's sleek side and murmured his goodbyes.

Then he turned to face the portal and walked through it.

99

Chapter 19

Lucifer, Michael, Gabriel, Beelzebub, Raphael, Uriel, and Zachriel were gathered in the council room.

"Both the Queen and the Matriarch may have promised peace, but I think some will not follow their lead." As Gabriel voiced his distress.

"I am fairly certain we will not see many, if any, of the griffins attempting to wage any form of war. My conversation with their Matriarch went very well. They have no desire to continue this war because of their losses. Their focus is to find the former Matriarch. I told them when we had angels to spare, we would aid them with that," Raphael reported, unaware of Azrael's recent deed.

"Yes, and what of the dragons? The Queen may desire peace, but some will follow Draaheson, and others will not conform to this notion of peace. It has been the case in the past," Gabriel pointed out.

"The Queen gave me her word that she will not wage war against us and will try to get her people to abide by her decree. We can't ask any more of her," Beelzebub spoke with a furrowed brow. "We have to expect that there will be dragons who wish to continue the fight. The question is how many."

"Perhaps we can get some of the griffins to aid us?" Zachriel suggested.

"No," Michael said. "That would create bad blood between the griffins and the dragons. Then we would have another war and be forced to choose a side."

"With the seizing of Amy, I suspect that some of the dragons may have aligned themselves with Mother Earth already. I spoke with the Queen, and she did not know about Amy or her abduction. I can think of no one else aside from

Mother Earth who would have reason to hold her," Beelzebub added.

"If Mother Earth and the dragons are behind it, I wonder if Mother Earth intends to part with her soil, regardless of whether Azrael passes the trials. It also tells us there is a divide among the dragons. We should not expect all of them to follow their Queen." Lucifer was thinking out loud. "We also do not know how many dragons would support Mother Earth."

Uriel leaned forward, intent and alert. "Then what would you have us do?"

"I think we may have to assemble an army to fight both the dragons and Mother Earth," Lucifer proposed.

Gabriel was deeply disturbed by the idea. "Fighting a species is one thing, but an entire world? We do not have the numbers to launch such an attack."

"We must prepare the largest army we have ever assembled. Every able angel must be involved. We need not defeat her; we only need the soil from the Water of Eternal Youth," Lucifer countered.

There was silence amongst the Seven. Each of them was in deep thought over such a grave task. Mother Earth's power was vast; even with billions of angels ready to fight, they would stand little chance of defeating her.

"Beelzebub, do you have any thoughts or insight to provide?" Lucifer asked.

"I am not convinced that putting an army on the Earth is a good idea. It may only anger her and cause a bigger battle than is needed. I feel Azrael will find a way to get her soil from her," Beelzebub answered.

"And if he does not? And the dragons are aiding Mother Earth?" Uriel posed.

"Then we should prepare for a large battle. But for now, I think we should heal, rest and think," Beelzebub replied.

"I agree with Beelzebub," Michael said.

"So do I." Lucifer stood.

The rest of the angels nodded their approval.

"Then it is settled. Rest, heal, and think. I will speak to Lilith and see if she can find any information on the dragons and whether Mother Earth is indeed aligned with them," Lucifer concluded.

Chapter 20

Draaheson and another ancient shön dragon called Zaar landed by the Water of Eternal Youth. Zaar was one of Draaheson's most loyal and powerful allies. He was only slightly below Draaheson in strength and power. But what he lacked there, he made up for in wits and agility. Waiting for the two massive creatures was Mother Earth.

She had the appearance of a twelve-year-old girl. Her physical form was made up of Earth's elements. Visible streams of water flowed through it like veins of blood. Her eyes glowed with an intense yellow and red fire. Her long curly hair constantly moved as though blown by the wind. Her voice gave the impression that it both echoed and came from underwater.

You spoke the truth. The queen has declared peace between our peoples, and the griffins have also stopped their attacks, Draaheson told her.

"Will you now pledge yourself to me?" she demanded.

Yes. We will join you in your fight against the angels. I have spoken to many of the griffins, and some will join us. How can you be so confident that there will be such a battle? The dragon asked.

"In the same way, I knew your queen would make peace with the angels. I have seen it. Remember, in joining me, you will listen to me and adhere to my plans as we discussed," Mother Earth declared.

Since you dwell here, I want to know how you will protect us from the Queen in Aeirliel. And your claim that the dragons will have a voice in the Heavens if we join you, when will this occur? Draaheson demanded.

"Draaheson, Be patient. I did not say I would protect you; I said you would be safe from her. And why would you fear her? You told me that over half the dragons would follow your lead. Is this a lie?" she challenged.

No! It is the truth. The dragons know who their true leader should be. I have well over half ready to continue the fight, he replied with resentment.

"That will be more than enough," Mother Earth assured him.

What shall we do about Azrael? He already completed one of your trials.

"You will do nothing. He may or may not finish the trials. Either way, I will not simply give away the soil that will inevitably cause my destruction."

Chapter 21

Amy lay unconscious on a large circular stone approximately ten feet in diameter. Around the stone was nothing but empty space. Aside from a few bruises, she was unharmed. The boom and shaking of footsteps awakened her. Her Angelic eyes adjusted to the dark and humid cave in moments. Unaware of where she was and trying to recall what had happened, she spoke the first thought that came to her mind.

"Azrael?"

Sitting up, she looked around and tried to assess her whereabouts. She moved to the edge of the circular stone but was knocked back by a green ward. "What is this place?" she asked, bewildered.

Your prison, a dark and cryptic voice echoed throughout her mind.

The stone floor shook as the dragon walked along the walls. As he moved, his massive shape, hidden in the shadows, became apparent to Amy. The cave had no visible light, but she could still see him with her Angelic eyes. As well as she could tell, the ancient fire dragon, Gronoch, could see even better. His purple scales looked as black as night, and his size was equal to that of Draaheson. He carried scars across his face and body. He refused to have them mended as he liked to show his enemies the numerous wounds he had taken, and that he had survived them. He was the perfect choice to watch over Amy, having single-handedly slain tens of thousands of angels in battle.

"Who are you? Where is Azrael?"

Who I am is not essential, Gronoch rumbled. *I don't know where your love is. But I would guess he is attempting the trials of Mother Earth.*

"Why did you take me?" Amy asked.

You are our insurance. We do not want Azrael to take the soil to God, and it appears Mother Earth feels the same.

Amy needed clarification. "But why? If he completes the trials, it means he is worthy. She has to give it to him."

Maybe she should, but that does not mean she will.

"Why would the dragons not want Azrael to take the soil from Mother Earth?" she asked.

We have seers in our society who have not seen good things for us with this new creation, Gronoch explained. *If you were told this creation could mean the loss of half of your species, would you not want to prevent it from happening?*

Gronoch leaped from one side of the cave wall to the other without making a sound. Amy saw him move but could not locate where he landed. "What kind of dragon are you?"

I am an ancient fire dragon, Gronoch said proudly.

Amy turned to where the voice was coming from. "Shouldn't you be red?"

The color and element of a dragon vary. Even though you are a young angel, you seem to know very little for a Seraphim.

"Excuse me, but not all of us know everything like Gabriel. Even though he really doesn't," she added in a mutter. "But I know the size of a dragon relates to how old it is. Oh! I know they can change or reduce their size too."

Very good. Perhaps you are not a complete waste. Not all of us can alter our size. Did you know we can change or shape?

"I read about it," she nodded. "Dragons are very powerful creatures and can do many things."

We can, and I have killed many angels.

Amy saw his eyes in the darkness. Though it scared her, she wanted to show him she was unafraid. "When Azrael gets here, he will kill you."

Gronoch's laugh caused a tremble in the cave. *He does not know where you are. No one does. And if he does find his way here, I welcome him to try where countless others have failed.*

Chapter 22

Azrael crested a hill and looked out over a flooded terrain. Scattered treetops stuck out of the water, but as he peered over the great distance with his angel eyes, he saw no end to the flood. His wings slid out of his back, and he flew over the waterlogged land.

Azrael came across a large pyramid-shaped structure as he glided through the air. When he got closer, he realized the structure was made of ice and water. He slid his hand along the surface as he flew around it. It parted through his fingers like water but still maintained its shape. He determined which side was the entrance to the structure and landed on the water-made staircase. When he landed, ice formed under his feet to support his weight. With each step he took, ice formed where the water had been. He ran his hands over the wall, hoping to find a door, but could not locate anything. He pulled some algae-based components from his pouch and placed them strategically along the wall. Finally, the edges of a door became clear. He used more of the algae, and the door opened.

He entered the vast building made of water and ice. The massive interior was mazelike, with many rooms and hallways that led to more rooms. Azrael entered one of these rooms and saw the phoenix contained in a cube of water. He took a small pebble from his pouch and threw it. It passed through the cube.

An illusion, he reasoned.

To test his suspicion, he levitated off the ground and cast a spell to make himself transparent. He floated into the room above the one where he now stood. He found the same illusion and realized that each of the tens of thousands of rooms contained the same trick.

Where is the true phoenix?

He floated back into the main entry room and hovered. As he contemplated the scenario, a prominent humanoid figure entered the room. The Matron Mother of the mermaids proudly stood before Azrael; she was at least half a foot taller than he. She was dressed in primitive clothing more fit for a jungle. With bright amber eyes and pale china skin, her thin muscular figure was draped with her long, wet, black hair. Mermaids were capable of having legs when they desired.

In most cases, it was when they were out of the water, such as now. But while in water, they were far more powerful and would revert their legs to a fish-like tail. She narrowed her eyes at Azrael.

"Come to strip me of my prize?" she accused.

Azrael chose his words carefully. "You say that as though the phoenix belongs to you. I am not here as a thief. I am here as a liberator."

The Matron Mother smirked. "Why not come to the ground, angel?"

"I know a few things about mermaids. Touching the water would give you the power to pull me into the depths. I will not give you that chance."

"An educated angel. If that is the case, perhaps I will allow you an opportunity to obtain the phoenix, if you can solve my riddles. But be warned, Gabriel's brilliant mind could not solve the puzzles I presented."

Azrael hesitated for a moment. He thought it must have been Michael, not Gabriel, who failed this challenge. The Matron Mother was right about one thing; Gabriel's mind was one of the greatest, if not the greatest, in all the Heavens. But he could not doubt himself, not now. With Amy missing, there was no time to waste on uncertainty. "Very well."

"Let's start with something simple." She walked around him as she spoke. "The more you take, the more you leave behind."

"You are right. It is simple. The answer is footsteps. The more you take, the more you leave behind," Azrael quickly responded.

"Very good. I shall give you something more challenging test since this was too easy for a clever mind like yours."

Azrael was indeed brighter than the Matron Mother gave him credit for. Even as they spoke, he used a transparent version of himself to search all the rooms to see if the phoenix was in this structure. For all he knew, she could be lying, and the phoenix was not even here. Or she could lie about giving him the phoenix. Azrael was not taking any chances on something so important. He cast a spell over each phoenix he encountered, and when it glowed white, he knew it was an illusion.

The Matron Mother strolled around him. He was careful to keep a reasonable distance from her reach.

"Let's try this one. When one does not know what it is, then it is something, but when one knows what it is, then it is nothing. I will give you three guesses on this riddle."

"White lies?"

"No. A little more difficult than the first?" she asked, delighting in his struggle.

"Yes, it is."

Azrael paused momentarily to show he was thinking and buy him the time he needed to find the phoenix. "Is it an untold truth?"

"No. One more guess."

One more guess would be all he needed. He already knew the answer; he needed more time to search the structure.

He had searched hundreds of rooms and still found nothing. "Is the answer a riddle?"

"Yes," she replied with disappointment as she scowled at him. "You are a clever one, aren't you? Now for my last and most difficult riddle. Ready?"

"I shall do my best."

"A white dove flew down by the castle. Along came a king and picked it up handless, ate it up toothless, and carried it away wingless. Once again, I shall give you three guesses."

"White roses that are wilting away?" he asked.

"No."

Again, he paused to give the impression that he was thinking long and hard about his answers. "Paper being torn into pieces?"

"Wrong again. One more guess."

"Wait, I think I know the answer. Is it snow melting away by the sun?"

"Yes, it is," she replied with anger. "But I will not let you have the phoenix."

Azrael was unsurprised by her response, yet he still needed to know if the phoenix was here. He had nearly searched the entire structure.

"But I answered your riddles correctly," he protested.

"Now, I must answer a riddle from you. If I answer it, you will not get the phoenix. If I fail to answer it, I give you the phoenix."

"How do I even know the phoenix is here?" Azrael asked.

"It is here. Mother Earth would not allow me to put it any other place."

"Do I have your word that you will give it to me?"

"Yes," the Matron Mother responded.

"All right, give me a moment to think of a good one."

He knew she had no intention of giving him the magical bird. He finally reached the last set of rooms and cast the same spell. This time the eyes of the phoenix grew bright red, and Azrael smiled. "I think I have a challenge for you. How many guesses are you allowed?" he queried.

"Three."

"All right. I never was, and am always to be. No one ever saw me, nor ever will. And yet I am the confidence of all to live and breathe on this terrestrial ball. What am I?"

"The sun," she said confidently.

"No."

"Is it hope?" the Matron Mother suggested, still unfazed.

"No. One more guess."

The Matron Mother was frustrated and angry with Azrael. She could not hide it any longer. He was cautious and watchful of her movements.

"Is it the future?"

"Close, but no. I am afraid that those are all of your guesses. Will you take me to the phoenix?"

"No! I will not. You will tell me the answer and give me another riddle."

Azrael shook his head. "I will tell you the answer. But I am afraid I cannot give you another riddle."

"Then you will never see your precious phoenix."

"I think you had no intention of giving me the phoenix," Azrael reasoned.

She glared at him. "Fight me in combat, and if you defeat me, I will give it to you."

"I am not here to fight you. I am here to restore the balance of life and death in this land. The answer is…tomorrow."

The transparent Azrael released the phoenix when he spoke the word tomorrow. The water prison around the phoenix melted, and the entire structure began to shake and collapse. The sun burst through the clouds, and the water across the land started to melt away. The phoenix shot out from its prison and flew away into the sky.

Azrael, still hovering from the spell he had used, unfolded his wings as the structure around him disintegrated. "Farewell."

He flapped his wings and lifted in the air. The Matron Mother leaped off an ice-made statue and tried to claw and grab him but missed by a hair.

"Curse you, angel," she muttered under her breath. "I will learn more of you and have my revenge."

She sank into the depths of the waters, her legs turning into the tail of a fish. She quickly flowed through a river that led back to the ocean before the water on land disappeared.

The land slowly returned to the state it had once been in. A small river ran through the vast tropical valley. Rich fruits blossomed once again on trees. Flowers of various colors and forms bloomed, and the land was healthy for animals to return. Azrael landed softly on the grass of a nearby hill and observed the beauty returning to the terrain.

The freed phoenix flew over to him. It shrank to a small size and doused its flames to rest on his arm. As she rested on his forearm, her color morphed from bright red and yellow to soft blue and purple. She curled up next to Azrael and snuggled into his chest to thank him. Azrael heard the phoenix's voice in his head.

"You are welcome, my friend," he assured her. "Go now; you are free."

The phoenix flew into the sky and changed back to its former colors. It enlarged its body to nearly double the size of the angel. She shrieked out a long call that echoed throughout the land and flew over the valley. A shimmering white and blue portal opened beside Azrael.

"And now for the last of my trials, Azrael," Mother Earth spoke.

He was happy about the deed he had done. For him, it was not just about besting the Matron Mother or completing the trials. He was pleased because he felt he had done a good thing for the creatures of Earth. Azrael felt more confident about his abilities. He readied himself and walked into the portal.

Chapter 23

In the Seventh Heaven, all was calm and quiet. Michael stood on the palace balcony overlooking the glorious city of angels. Angels sat in chariots attached to winged horses. The Kingdom glistened in the soft golden-tinted light as the angel's day ended. Michael reflected on the events that had transpired and those that had yet to be.

Will God's creation of mortals help end all of this madness, or will it worsen matters? He thought and closed his eyes to peer into the future. He could not see a clear outcome; perhaps His creation would hinder and help. The future seemed so uncertain with the mortals. But maybe Lucifer could see this future.

Michael wondered what things would be like if Lucifer had not been there to save him countless times. He was a true leader and an inspiration to all the angels. Though Michael tried to be like Lucifer, it was never his nature to give speeches or inspire through his words. Even Gabriel was more accomplished as a speaker. Michael was far more introverted and preferred to speak softly and privately to those around him. *Is that what a true leader does?* He asked himself. *Is that what my brothers and sisters expect from me?* He felt fortunate that all the angels' duties and responsibilities belonged to Lucifer and not to him. While he was a leader and would lead the angels in battles, he knew Lucifer was the one the angels looked to for guidance and support. Lucifer was an inspiration and a guiding light to everyone. He felt a strong presence enter the balcony behind him, and he knew it was Lucifer.

"How are you, Michael? You seem troubled." Lucifer touched Michael's shoulder gently.

"I've been thinking about a great many things."

"You are becoming more like Beelzebub in that sense," Lucifer suggested.

"No, I doubt I could ever think as much as he," Michael said with a dry laugh.

"No, perhaps not. But I believe you have as much wisdom as he does, if not more. I wish you would speak your mind more often."

"We cannot all be as bold as you, Lucifer. Maybe it is a good thing I am not. We might end up competing, and I fear I would lose too often."

They both chuckled.

Lucifer pretended to consider. "I would let you win now and again."

"Thanks for those words of encouragement." Michael's tone was sarcastic. Then he grew serious again. "I have just been thinking about the creation of the mortal."

"As was I. The Father seems to believe the mortal to be of great importance, maybe even more than us, my brother."

"Does that bother you?" Michael asked.

"Well...no..." Though it truly did bother Lucifer, more than he wanted to admit. The fact that he and his brothers and sisters were going to such lengths for one creation bothered him. Many more angels would die, and his heart bled for them, not understanding why so many should be sacrificed. Never before had he felt this uncertainty, this pain in his heart. What was so special about the humans? Surely, they would not be greater than he. He was the first creation of God and the most beloved. God selected angels to rule the Heavens and guard the universe He created. Knowing humans would be very much like them but would not have their gifts and abilities troubled Lucifer's mind and soul.

"You seem somewhat reluctant," Michael observed.

"I am the first, Michael. I fear He will put the mortals above us," he admitted.

"I doubt that He will love any one creation more than another. But would it be such a bad thing to have humans above us? Maybe they will change things so there will never again be wars between us, the dragons, griffins, or any other creation."

Lucifer shook his head. "Or maybe we will have more wars. You know what I am speaking of, Michael. I know you have gazed into the future as I have. I wish I could share in your optimism, but my heart is full of doubt."

"Do you hope that Azrael fails in his quest then?" Michael asked.

"Never," Lucifer responded immediately. "I want our little brother to fulfill the first steps to his destiny."

"Do not worry; he will fulfill his destiny," whispered a voice from the shadows.

Lilith became visible and pulled her hood back, displaying her beautiful face.

"Eavesdropping?" Lucifer asked.

"Actually, I just arrived. I only heard the end of the conversation."

Michael regarded her with interest. "What brings you here, Lilith?"

"To report some of my findings at Lucifer's request. It would appear that most of the dragons will not be following their Queen's decree. Draaheson is leading them, as we suspected. A sizable army of dragons and griffins now surrounds the Water of Eternal Youth. Jrindren observed Mother Earth and Draaheson planning the placement of their armies."

"We will need to ready every able-bodied angel and call for the jinn as well. Any help will be appreciated," Lucifer mused.

"Should we ask the Jinn to care for the duties of the angels? Are any of the others aware of this?" Michael asked.

Gathering her long blonde hair, Lilith drew it over her shoulder. "I have only told you two."

"Well, please inform the others. Have Israfel and Jrindren begin to gather the angels. And I want you to ask our Jinn cousins to take care of the Heavens and monitor the duties of the angels while we are away," Lucifer commanded.

"As you wish." Lilith bowed and disappeared.

The jinn were not as plentiful as the angels but shared the same responsibilities and had a similar structure of authority. Like the angels, all the jinn answered to the Heavenly Seven.

Michael was worried. "Our hope rests in Azrael's hands. We may be able to fight, but I do not know that we can win this."

"Take good heart, brother. We must look to others for aid. Perhaps if we go to small places, we will find big surprises. Send for Opal Eye," Lucifer added.

Chapter 24

Uriel was practicing with his bow and arrow. He stood in the courtyard's center, facing targets of different shapes and sizes arranged at various heights. He notched an arrow and let out a soft breath. In the blink of an eye, he unleashed fifteen arrows at all the targets. He allowed himself a self-satisfied grin. Raphael lay on the grass, leaning against a pillar. He was resting after numerous hours of healing and observing Uriel's display of skill.

"Pick a spot on any tree or target," Uriel ordered.

"You will hit it. I know, I know. You have done this many times and in many ways," Raphael replied with a lack of interest.

"And I will keep doing it to remind you. You can be forgetful." Uriel smirked as he notched another arrow.

Raphael was insulted. His senses became attentive as his body readied for combat. "I most certainly am not forgetful! Why I remember virtually every divine spell there is."

"I only jest," Uriel insisted.

"You are not funny," Raphael muttered, slumping back against the pillar.

Uriel launched arrows using great speed with each one he notched. One of the arrows grazed past Raphael and hit the target at the dead center. Raphael froze, and Uriel chuckled.

"Once again, you are not funny," Raphael insisted.

Then his outraged face relaxed as he laughed with Uriel. He knew his closest friend would never intentionally hit him, and he was too skilled for such an accident. But just as Uriel knew how to get under Raphael's skin, so too did Raphael know to do the same to his redheaded brother.

"We all know that you never miss and are the greatest archer in the Heavens. But as to who the greatest swordsman is, that is under debate," Raphael remarked with a grin.

Uriel leaned on the arc of his bow, and his face became solemn and stern. "I will have you know that just as I am the best bowman, I am also the best swordsman."

"Careful, Uriel, your face is almost as red as your hair," Raphael laughed.

"Raphael—" He began to argue but realized his friend was exacting his revenge for Uriel's earlier teasing and shook his head ruefully.

"That has always been the problem with your jokes, Raphael; you tend to be the only one laughing," observed a voice from the courtyard corner.

Two angelic warriors, Israfel and Jrindren, entered. Like Uriel, they were skilled fighters with two swords. They had a friendly competition millennium old to determine who among the angels was the greatest swordsman in the Heavens. Many other angels took part in the tournament. Michael, Beelzebub, Raziel, Sariel and others. The only one who did not participate was Azrael.

"Perhaps we should schedule another duel, Uriel," Israfel suggested.

"I did not know you liked being embarrassed so frequently," Uriel boasted.

Jrindren was not to be left out. "You may have lost a step or two over the past few centuries, but I would still entertain a duel with you."

"I have no problem embarrassing two of my brothers," Uriel's eyes lit up. "Remember, there will be a line to compete with me."

"How about we include Raziel and the other angels," Raphael murmured. "Make a big spectacle of the whole thing."

There was nothing Uriel enjoyed more than a competition. "You are filled with good ideas. You can be one of the judges and we can have a second Tournament of the swordsmen."

"I was not volunteering," Raphael held up his hands.

"As for you two, I would be more than happy to simultaneously appease both of you in a duel." Uriel dropped his bow and drew both swords from where they hung on his sides. He whirled them around in a dazzling display.

"What if Azrael participated?" Raphael asked.

Israfel raised an eyebrow. "I would welcome the chance to duel him."

"Well, nothing, never mind. I have said too much as it is."

"Azrael would be a welcome opponent. Especially considering what he is to become," Jindren declared.

"I am afraid we are going to have to wait for these contests of swords for some time," Israfel announced, returning at last to the serious nature of their visit.

"Thank the Heavens. But why?" Raphael asked.

"We have news that may make you wish we were going to have the distraction of the duels, Raphael," Israfel said.

Raphael did not catch on to the change in Israfel's tone. "Gabriel is going to give another speech?"

The group chuckled.

"Not quite," Jindren said sternly. "It is much more serious than that."

Chapter 25

On Earth, an enormous force of dragons had spread out in a valley near the Water of Eternal Youth. They had placed themselves strategically in the air and on the ground, including a small force of griffins. Draaheson oversaw the army from the knoll.

We are prepared. The angel Lilith went to the Angelic as you said she would. Zaar landed beside him and reported.

She is a fool if she genuinely believes we cannot see through her invisibility spell. The Angelic do not stand a chance against the Earth and us, should they be foolish enough to come here, Draaheson reasoned.

The angel Amy is under guard, and no one has attempted to rescue her, Zaar added.

Good. Gronoch will be more than a match for any who find her.

And if they do not find her? Zaar asked.

She is there to ensure that Mother Earth does not give the soil to Azrael and that he does not give the soil to God. Should he want to see her alive, he must abandon his quest for the soil, Draaheson explained.

But Mother Earth has no intention of giving him the soil. Why should you worry about that?

Draaheson turned his head to Zaar. *Despite her insistence that she will not give it to him, I have doubts. I will be the one to prevent the creation of the mortal.*

Chapter 26

The Kingdom of the Fey was situated on an island called Egressa. Bright violets, vivid crimsons, gold, and silver dominated the land. The colors were alive on various lush green exotic flowers, mushrooms, and trees. The realm felt foreign in comparison to the rest of Aeirliel.

Opal Eye and Beelzebub stood in front of three tiny lights. One of the lights was Bien, king of the Fey. Bien was an older man with a white beard that grazed his chest. He was dressed conservatively for a Fey; he revealed no skin besides his hands and face. Bien, like Opal Eye, chose to age as time passed. The two were old friends. Bien entrusted Opal Eye with the task of watching over his numerous daughters away from the Kingdom of the Fey. For many centuries, and sometimes for their entire lives, Fey women had high hormone levels and were quick to attempt to lure in partners. Bien did not want his daughters to be so careless, and he had Opal Eye monitor them until he felt they were of the right age to return to their homeland.

"I understand the predicament the Angelic is in, Opal Eye. However, I do not think I can endanger my kingdom like this," Bien explained.

"Lucifer would not ask for your help unless the situation was dire."

"We are no match for the dragons or Mother Earth. They are too powerful. I am surprised the Angelic have lasted as long as they have against the dragons and griffins. Besides, it is the Angelic who are the guardians of Paradise, not the Fey."

"Even we must call for aid at times. We have many angels wounded and unable to help in the coming battle." Opal Eye pleaded for him to understand.

128

"With so many other beings to choose from, why choose the small Fey?" Bien wondered.

"Sometimes the largest and most powerful creations don't notice small beings or think they can be a real threat. The Fey have been known to slay dragons," Opal Eye pointed out.

"Yes, we have killed a fair share of dragons, though we are usually underestimated. Our numbers are far beyond that of the Angelic and the dragons. Though, it is unlikely that we can help end this war. It has been going on for centuries."

"Bien, the war between Angelic, griffins, and dragons is over. We are enlisting your aid only to help Azrael get the soil from the Earth," Beelzebub interjected.

"Yes, to create these mortals. Have you seen what dark things they will bring to the universe?" Bien worried. "Perhaps we should be coming to the aid of Mother Earth."

"For every piece of darkness, there is a piece of light," Beelzebub reassured him.

"I have always liked you, Beelzebub. You always paint a fair picture of things. It was smart of you to bring this one with you, old friend," Bien said to Opal Eye.

"Then you are going to help us?" Opal Eye pressed.

"Yes, we will. But I will only be taking a portion of our army. They will have to volunteer. I will not force this on my people."

"Thank you, old friend," Opal Eye said. "We shall speak with Lucifer and begin our preparations."

"I will go with you. I am sure that I can offer some input." Bien turned to one of his generals. "Let all know of our plans and my request. Ready our armies to the north and west. Tell them the Fey will be going to battle."

Chapter 27

Amy stood alone in the cold, dark cave. The green ward was still present though it could not be seen with the naked eye unless she bumped into it. She walked toward the general area she had determined was the border, with her mind in deep thought. *What did Beelzebub tell Azrael?* she thought to herself. *The best way through magic...no, that's not how it went.*

She paused, considering, and then she lit up. *Sometimes the best way around magic is through it.*

She reached out and touched the ward; her hand went through to the other side. Excited, she retracted her hand. *Now, I must awaken my wings.*

Amy pushed her wings upward and out, but agony ripped across her shoulders and down her back. She gasped and stumbled backward. Waiting for the pain to recede, she caught her breath and gathered all her determination and courage.

When she thought she was ready, she rose and pulled her arms into her body, pressing her wings against the skin of her back even more forceful than before. This time the pain knocked her to the floor. She cried out as tears filled her eyes. She had not realized anything could hurt that much. She put her head on her knees and wept. *I am foolish and useless.*

Poor angel. Too painful, is it? I knew that you would not try to escape. That ward is for any who try to free you, not to prevent you from escaping, Gronoch's voice echoed through the dismal cave.

Amy saw the red eyes of the dragon moving along the walls and straightened her spine. "I'll find a way."

You know too little of magic and need to gain skill with a blade. Even if you did escape, you would be no match for me, Gronoch rumbled.

"Sometimes you need more than magic and skill with a blade," Amy challenged.

And what would that be? he asked lazily.

"Love."

The dragon gave a thundering chuckle. *Love? It will take more than that to defeat me.*

While Amy knew it took skill with a sword and knowledge of magic to defeat an ancient dragon. She believed love was what separated Azrael from all other angels. Yes, he was skilled with a sword, as was Uriel. Yes, he understood magic, as did Beelzebub. But he was more than an angel with skill, knowledge, and power. The love in his heart made him who he was; that was how she knew he was the one the prophecies spoke about. It was also how she knew he would be the one to save her.

131

Chapter 28

Azrael moved through the forest, observing everything around him. He did not know what the Trial of Death would be, so he could not prepare for it. As he moved under some low-hanging tree branches, he heard a whimpering. He moved through the forest and traced the origin of the sound. He stopped in shock when he found it. It was his black unicorn friend who had aided him. Azrael rushed to the unicorn's side and cast a spell over it to see what was wrong.

"Hold on, my friend. You have been poisoned. I will try to help you," he said, running his hands through the poor beast's mane to soothe it.

He cast another spell to counteract the poison. It worked briefly, then the toxin seemed to change its nature and surpassed the magic. The new poison raced through the unicorn's body. Azrael cast another spell but got the same result.

Mother Earth appeared behind him. "This is your final trial, Azrael. Your friend has been poisoned with one of the most lethal toxins on Earth. It kills over the course of many hours, sometimes days, and is extremely painful. This is only the first stage of the poison. It is nowhere near as painful as it will become."

"I don't know how to help him. The poison is unlike anything I have encountered. I think only Raphael would be able to help him."

"You are correct. He would be one of the few capable of understanding the workings of this poison. But you must make a choice. Will you end his life now to save him from this pain, or will you let him suffer through the pain before he dies, so that he may experience true suffering?"

Azrael thought quickly and stroked the neck of his close friend. He could not bear to watch him suffer. He knew that Mother Earth was referring to the law written by God that stated all creatures experienced some form of suffering so that they might appreciate the good things that came to them. Why should this brave unicorn be forced to suffer a painful death? Azrael knew that he would fail this test. He did not feel he should go against what he believed for the sake of passing a trial. If he did, then everything would be a lie. He had to make this choice with honesty in his heart; that was something he valued within himself. He realized he might disappoint his older brothers with his failure but had to stay true to himself. He looked into the eyes of the unicorn as he grimaced in pain. Water dripped from the animal's eyes. One word came to Azrael's mind as he saw this unicorn. He saw the pain and agony and knew his friend had already suffered.

Mercy. He shut his eyes.
"A being once told me to follow what the love in your heart tells you."

"What does it say to you, Azrael?" Mother Earth questioned.

Azrael shut his eyes tightly. "I wish for his suffering to end now."

"He will not know true suffering. It will end before he experiences the real pain of the poison."

Azrael gazed into the eyes of Mother Earth. "If it is my choice, then I choose to end his suffering."

"Very well."

Mother Earth sank into the ground and rose next to the unicorn. She placed her hand on the animal. A slight glow came from her hand, and the unicorn closed his eyes.

Azrael stroked the unicorn's neck. "I am so sorry, my friend. Please forgive me." His azure eyes streaked with tears.

The unicorn let out one last breath and closed his eyes forever. Azrael's heart was filled with pain at losing his friend. After the unicorn had helped and protected him, all he could do in his time of need was end the pain and allow him to die.

"Come with me, Azrael." Mother Earth opened a portal and sank into the ground.

"Goodbye," Azrael said to the unicorn and followed her.

****

He emerged from the portal at the Water of Eternal Youth with Mother Earth standing before him.

"You have passed all three of my trials," she said serenely.

Her statement surprised him. "I did not think I passed. You seemed not to agree with my choice."

"All creatures will go through some form of suffering in the course of their lives. That unicorn may not have suffered to the degree that most creatures do. At that moment, it did suffer."

"It was my choice to free him from that," Azrael said slowly. "It was my choice to grant him mercy."

A merciful angel. She was surprised to hear this word. While she knew angels were compassionate, it always seemed that justice and righteousness were more typical of them.

"Yes, and your choice was the right one. You are much different from your Angelic brothers. But I will not be giving you my soil."

"I passed your trials," he protested.

"I will not give it to you; your brothers and sisters will come with an army to take it. But I am more than ready for

134

them. I have the aid of the dragons and the griffins in addition to my army," Mother Earth told him.

"You are willing to wage war over this?"

"I am willing to do what I must to prevent the destruction of this planet," she said grimly.

It was not only the planet but her own destruction she was preventing. She saw what was in store for her.

Chapter 29

In the outer valley of the Water of Eternal Youth, the Heavenly Seven and Opal Eye rode to the cusp of a hill. Lucifer pulled the reigns back on his black mount and stopped. His six brothers and Opal Eye trotted up next to him. They looked miles ahead with their Angelic eyes to see the force of dragons and griffins. Tens of thousands of dragons covered the ground and hovered in the air.

"We shall attack from four sides as planned," Lucifer reminded them.

Raphael was astonished. "I did not think so many would oppose the Queen's decree."

"Do not forget the force from the Earth," Uriel pointed out.

Zachriel looked grim. "We all knew the dangers of this battle. We should get to our positions and prepare for the confrontation."

"Perhaps someone should say something before we proceed," Michael suggested as he glanced toward Lucifer.

The other angels followed his gaze.

Lucifer did not look; he knew they all looked to him for such a speech. "Very well," Lucifer said. He stretched out his mighty white wings and flew into the air. Lucifer looked down at an Angelic force so large that mortal eyes could not see the end. This was only one-fourth of the entire army. The three other divisions covered all directions of the water of eternal life at a great distance behind him, to his left and right. Each of these four armies was vast, and they could see Lucifer high up in the sky. Though his voice could carry a great distance, he spoke to them telepathically.

My brothers and sisters, today I must ask you to go beyond anything you have done in previous wars.

He flew to the army's rear and circled to the second position. *I need more than your courage, more than your skill with swords or bows, more than your knowledge of the magics.* Lucifer soared past the third army. *To win this battle, I need the love in your hearts and the compassion in your souls.* He soared over the last division of the army. *This battle cannot be won by the efforts of one or a few. All of you must win it. I need you to be at my side. With your courage and strength, we will unite and create a new era of peace. Together we must fight, and together, we shall win!*

He flew throughout each group to make sure everyone saw him up close.

The angels cheered in response.

Lucifer drew his mighty claymore sword. The blade shimmered in the sunlight. "For the Kingdom!" he shouted across the valley, and his voice echoed.

The angels drew their weapons and held them up. They all cheered.

He flew down low to the angels as they continued their cheers and touched some of their outstretched hands.

"LU-CI-FER! LU-CI-FER! LU-CI-FER!" chanted the angels from all four corners of the soon-to-be battlefield. The chants echoed throughout the land.

He returned to his horse as the chants and cheers continued.

"Fine speech. How many times did you practice it, I wonder?" Beelzebub asked with a grin.

"Quiet, Beelzebub," Michael snapped. "It was a good speech."

"Thank you, Michael. Let's all take our positions."

Zachriel and Gabriel rode off to the left.

"I am glad some of us are eager to start," Raphael muttered.

"Greet them with a ready sword, or you may find yourself in need of healing my friend." Beelzebub patted Raphael on the shoulder and rode off with Opal Eye.

Raphael let out a sigh. "Lucifer's speech was considerably more inspiring, Beelzebub."

He and Uriel cantered away.

"And you, Lucifer, are you inspired for today's conflict?" Michael asked.

"I am not so much inspired as I am confident."

"Why is that?"

"Regardless of what we may or may not do here, the day will be ours, but not because of us. It will be ours because Azrael will fulfill his destiny."

He signaled with a bright glow from his hand for the angels to move forward. Michael and Lucifer started down the hill toward the dragon army. Behind them, a great wave of angels took to the air, and others followed in formation on foot, on horses, or on winged horses in the air followed.

Chapter 30

Azrael hovered high in the air and observed the armies arrayed against each other. Mother Earth was on the ground, and though it appeared that she could not make out the battlefield from where she stood, she could see everything.

Sick with dismay, Azrael stood helpless. All of the trials he had passed would be for nothing if this battle had unfolded as it promised to do. It could lead to a war that would last longer than any other in the history of the universe.

"Please," he pleaded with Mother Earth, "you can stop this from happening. Honor your word and give me the soil."

"I cannot," she responded coldly.

The army of dragons, earth elementals, fire elementals, water elementals, and air elementals were formed around them. They were as great in number as the angels and Mother Earth could generate more if these fell. United with the dragons, the army of Earth pushed outward to greet the Angelic army.

The angels moved forward toward the dragons. Raphael was nervous about the coming battle, and Uriel saw it on his face.

"Have no fear, my friend. You have Heaven's greatest warrior at your side," Uriel assured him.

Israfel rode up beside them. "That is still under debate," he reminded Uriel.

Raphael nodded. Even knowing he could die today, he was comforted because he was with his friends and brothers. He knew they would be at his side and fight with him until the end. But it was neither the battle nor his death that made him fearful; it was the thought of how many angels would be wounded or killed. He was worried that he might be overwhelmed by their enemies and unable to use his healing powers. "I have the greatest friend at my side and could ask for nothing more," he told Uriel.

The four groups of angels picked up speed as the dragons and creatures of the Earth marched toward them.

Beelzebub and Jrindren raced in on their horses, angels charging behind them in the air and across the ground. Beelzebub drew his sword and motioned forward with it. A swarm of arrows whooshed over the two angel warriors and briefly darkened the sky above them. The arrows hit oncoming dragons but did little to slow or stop them. Beelzebub chanted a spell, and his free hand became charged with blue electricity. He projected his electric-filled hand at a dragon that was seconds away from pouncing on him. The lightning bolt shredded through the dragon, tearing off half its wing. The dragon landed head-first against a large rock. If the lightning bolt had not killed it, its neck snapping in two would have.

Beelzebub whispered in his horse's ear, shot out his black wings, and leaped into the air. He soared under and around dragons until he closed in on his target—one of the oldest and largest. He pierced the dragon's side with his sword and flew down to cut it open. The dragon squirmed at the cut and whipped his tail at Beelzebub. He carefully avoided the strike and bent in and around the tail. He spun midair and fired multiple small white orbs at the dragon.

The creature avoided some of the orbs and shot a breath of acid at Beelzebub. The white orbs did little harm to the dragon, but Beelzebub was not looking to kill it; he wanted to use its strength and power against its comrades and succeeded. He easily avoided the acid breath, but the two dragons behind him were less fortunate. They were engulfed in acid and collided. They smashed into the ground, crushing fire and earth elementals upon their landing.

141

Jrindren also dismounted his horse and quickly took down multiple creatures made of rock and water with his twin blades. He never liked to use magic unless he had to. He preferred to beat his foes in fair combat. But he knew that to defeat the creatures of earth, he would have to use more than a sword. He had asked Lilith to give him an enchanted amulet to alter the magical properties of his blades each time he struck a different element type. He quickly blitzed through water and air elementals with precision and speed. When his blades struck at them, they caused the creatures to freeze and slowed them. Jrindren slammed his blades into the ground and shattered his enemies; heat swelled from his blades and melted all the pieces.

In the distance, Opal Eye confidently stood with a staff in one hand. On a rock in front of him was Bien. Behind them was the immense army of the Fey. They covered the ground like ants on food. Their soldiers wore armor made of leather or thick hide that hugged their bodies but allowed free movement. It was less sophisticated than the Angelic. However, it was sturdy enough for the type of combat they entered. It covered the vital parts of their bodies but nothing more. Their weapons were primarily spears and other non-metallic objects. Some of the Fey had weapons and armor forged by the Angelic.

Amid the battle, huge water and fire elementals towered over the angels. Lilith flew near a group of fire elementals and radiated a spell of cold that shot out like a spinning cone of ice from her hands. Steam rose in the air as the ice hit the fire elementals. The smoke clouded up the area around them. One of the fire elementals collided with a water elemental. The two fell to the ground and merged to form a lava creature, its entire body of hot magma. It dripped pieces of lava, and angels had to scurry away to avoid the pieces. The lava creature threw balls of magma at the angels. Most could avoid the large balls, yet small pieces broke off and hit several angels unaware. They screamed

142

in pain as the lava melted their wings and burned their bodies, and they descended to the ground. The lava creature threw a massive chunk of magma. Lilith quickly put up a green energy shield that protected a group of angels from being melted away.

To her right, countless arrows lodged into a smaller dragon's head, neck, and chest, killing it. The dragon collapsed to the ground and was stepped on by a gigantic earth elemental. Lucifer and Michael swooped through the air over the fallen dragon as they battled a swift and brawny griffin. The griffin shot multiple lines of energy at the two angels. They wove around the blasts until a blast hit Michael's shield and knocked him out of the sky.

Michael spun as he fell. He crashed into a large earth elemental, which helped slow his descent. His body was bruised, and the earth elemental attacked him before he recovered and regained his senses. He rolled out of the way and flipped himself up in the air without using his arms. The earth elemental pummeled Michael with his fists. The angel quickly projected a spell to block the blows. The magic absorbed the impact, and the sheer force knocked Michael back several feet. A water elemental hit Michael on his flank, but he recovered to block multiple strikes from the being.

At the same time, the griffin assaulted Lucifer with numerous and rapid strikes, but he parried the talon with his long claymore sword. Still, the griffin scored a large gash on Lucifer's body. The wound began to heal as quickly as it was made. Lucifer's eyes flared white with anger, and he punched the griffin in the head. He pulled on its wing, leaped, and sprang off of it. He then turned around to launch a fireball in quick succession. The griffin could not wholly avoid the fireball; its entire left side was swallowed up in flame. The griffin nearly collided with a dragon in the air, but the dragon avoided it and batted it down toward the ground. Lucifer kept one eye out for Michael as he flew and fought.

Meanwhile, Michael was throwing a dagger at a water elemental. It had no immediate effect. It barreled toward him. As it did, it slowly evaporated, and the blade fell uselessly at the angel's feet. Michael stood but was slammed to the ground by Lucifer. A line of fire scorched past the two. Both were quick to their feet. They telepathically spoke to each other and coordinated how to attack the dragon. Michael and Lucifer sprang up and flew in different directions. They wove in and around the dragon, landing strikes with their swords while avoiding attacks.

The battle raged on with casualties on all sides. Angels, elements, dragons, and griffins collided in a bloody and violent dance. Arrows zinged across the battlefield. Even from a great distance, the spells of lightning and breaths of acid could be seen. It was complete chaos as dragons and angels fell to their deaths from the sky.

Chapter 31

Azrael was struck by the difference between the destructive conflict he watched rage to the calm setting where he stood by the Water of Eternal Youth. He floated in the air with Mother Earth standing beside him, unable to look away from the scenes of death. He wanted to aid his brothers and sisters in this conflict. He knew that was not his battle. His battle was at his side, and if he could prevail, it would end the chaos raging across Earth.

"Please stop this. There is no need for it. I did not come here to fight."

"You came for my soil, just as they have," she reprimanded him.

"Yes, you refuse to give it to me. Why?" Azrael asked.

"Because it will cause terrible pain. I have seen a glimpse of the future. You wish to rob me of it so the Father can use it to create the mortal. The mortal will then rob me of the living creatures of this world. The devastation caused by them will be far beyond the death toll in this battle."

"This is what God asked of me," he said.

Mother Earth faced Azrael. "Search the future, Azrael. You will see the sorrow mortals will bring to me. They will also bring sorrow to Him, the kingdom of the Heavens, Earth, Aeirliel—even to you."

"I have seen some of it," Azrael informed her. "They will also bring joy. The mortal will not dwell in this world. They will be in Aeirliel."

"I am afraid it will not always be so. I like you, young Azrael. You're not like most angels." She complimented him.

"Oh? And what are most angels like?"

146

"Most angels are too lawful. Take your Gabriel and Zachriel."

"Not all angels are like them. Michael is not. Nor is Lucifer."

Mother Earth hid her thoughts beneath heavy lids. "I feel angels believe themselves to be untouchable and immortal."

"We are neither. We have ageless bodies with a soul. But like anything else, we can be destroyed," Azrael reminded her.

"You should remind your Seven of that. Sometimes I feel they forget their humility. It may be too late now," Mother Earth warned him.

"End this battle," Azrael pleaded. "There is no need for more blood to be spilled."

Mother Earth turned her conflicted eyes onto the battlefield. Her fire red and yellow eyes burned with intense anger, and now a touch of saddened blue crept within them.

Chapter 32

Opal Eye's long gray hair and beard flowed in the breeze as he firmly grasped his staff. He studied the progress of the battle carefully. He slowly moved his head to the right and looked down. Opal Eye nodded to Bien, and he returned the gesture. Bien leaped off the rock and shot a small light into the air. Hundreds of thousands of fey on the ground readied themselves at the sight of the light.

Opal Eye started to chant the words of a spell. Each of the fey began to glow with a blue aura. The blue aura faded from sight as he completed the final words to the enchantment.

Bien drew his sword. "To war!"

The fey shouted and raised their weapons. The army flew into the air and swarmed past Opal Eye. The fey blanketed the sky, blocking the sun like the army was a horde of locusts.

Opal Eye staggered and leaned on his staff as the army passed. The spell had drained him of much of his energy. Even he, Opal Eye, the eighth angel of creation, must recover before he rushes in to join the battle. The countless fey flying obscured his vision, limiting his ability to join the anarchy.

Beelzebub fought on foot with his black wings out. He fought with precision, agility, and a significant level of calm. Foes from Earth fell to his left and to his right with little apparent effort on his part. He blocked a fire elemental with a spell and pierced its face with his sword. His blade glowed blue, and the creature sizzled into vapor. An earth elemental immediately attacked, but Beelzebub dodged the blow and flipped over the creature's arm. As he landed on the other side of it, he decapitated the earth elemental without turning around. Beelzebub continued to dispatch creatures of all four elements across the battlefield. His combat prowess had no equal, and his skill was magnificent to observe.

A shön dragon swooped down toward the evasive Beelzebub and slashed at him with its giant claw. Beelzebub turned to avoid it through instinct or simple luck and stabbed the dragon's claw. In a swift effort, he shifted his body, placed his free hand on the dragon's claw, and used the force of the blow in conjunction with his own sheer strength to hurl the mighty beast over his shoulder into a mountain-sized earth elemental. The dragon crashed into the stomach of the earth elemental and broke it in half. Beelzebub did not pause; he lept and sheathed his sword, throwing the dragon hundreds of yards into the air. His eyes flared with a white, and he pressed his hands together until a white glow circled them. A white beam burst between his palms and shot into the crippled shön dragon. The energy burned white-hot and disintegrated the beast instantly, causing an explosion that sent a gust rushing outward. Not content with his rampage of destruction, Beelzebub teleported rapidly across the battlefield, delivering strikes wherever possible.

Meanwhile, Jrindren and ten other angels battled a colossal griffin. The griffin swung its claw at five angels, but each of them broke formation in different directions to avoid the strike. A dragon came up from behind and scooped up two of the angels in her mouth. It tried to toss them into other angels, but only one was flung out. The less fortunate of the two got stuck between her teeth. She crunched her mouth closed, and the angel's blood gushed over the dragon's tongue.

Jrindren nose-dived at the dragon. It caught him in midair before he could land a blow of revenge. It threw him to the ground, severely injuring his shoulder. The dragon dove after him and landed on its legs before Jrindren. It brought its claw down on him, but a swarm of what appeared to be gnats amassed in front of the dragon. The dragon roared in rage and blew steam out of his nose. A group of fey entered the massive dragon's ears. It writhed around in anger and growled in pain. The fey guided the dragon toward another and rammed head first into the back of the knees of the other dragon. The two dragons crashed to the ground, and angels sprang at the opportunity to slay them. They shoved their spears through the beasts' vital organs and pierced the dragons' skulls. Yet the two dragons still managed to kill a few angels with their claws as they squirmed around.

The fey flew around dragons and griffins, sometimes to distract them and other times to lead them to their deaths. The fey was protected by the spell Opal Eye had placed around them and could take some of the blows and attacks projected by the dragons. But Opal Eye's spell could only withstand so much, and it eventually faded. The initial surprise and quickness of the fey aided them in taking down many dragons and griffins. A dragon shot a cone of acid at the flank of a group. Some could avoid the melting liquid, but many were covered in it, and shrieks of pain from the dying creatures emanated for nearly a mile.

Elsewhere, Lucifer was caught up in fighting the elements of fire and water. Several water elementals cut him, but his wounds healed instantly. He teleported to avoid various attacks and caused the fire and water elements to hurt each other instead. Lucifer cut down a number of the elements with his long claymore sword. He cared little for his wellbeing and stepped in front of what would have been deathblows to some of his fellow angels. Lucifer was burned severely by some fire elementals, but again, they healed instantly.

He shot a massive energy blast at the fire elementals, and all were extinguished. A water elemental launched sharp spikes of ice at him. Michael stepped in front of the shards and blocked them with his shield. Lucifer looked over his shoulder and sent a quick smile and nod of thanks to his younger brother. Michael returned the smile, and the two brothers arranged themselves back-to-back against the elements of the Earth.

Michael's fighting style was not elaborate or extraordinary, but it was effective. He was generic in his attacks and blocks. He was indeed a master of his craft. Lucifer's style was not as careful or clean and didn't need to be. Lucifer was willing to sacrifice a few cuts and blows to his body to get a killing blow to his opponent.

A gigantic dragon plunged toward the brothers and shot a line of electricity down at them. Lucifer saw the current out of the corner of his eye. "Michael, get down!"

He pushed his brother to the ground, away from danger, and prepared to sacrifice himself to save Michael's life. A green shield appeared around Lucifer and Michael and blocked the electricity. Lilith floated a hundred feet above them. Lucifer looked up to see her blast a ball of blue energy at the dragon. The dragon blocked the energy. Lucifer had already recovered and sprung into the air, using his long blade to puncture the vicious dragon.

In another part of the battlefield, Uriel spun his swords as he cut down water and earth elementals. He was both skilled and firm in his movements. While Beelzebub tended to avoid attacks, Uriel would make them happen. He was always the aggressor, seeking to make a kill or crippling blow to his enemies. Folded across his back was his bow. His quivers were carefully tucked away and shrunk in size to carry without encumbering his movements. As he progressed through the battle, Uriel had not yet suffered a wound—not even a scratch. He was not just a warrior but *the* warrior of the Heavens.

A dragon lunged toward him and snapped its jaw at him, but he avoided it. Uriel shoved his sword up through the bottom of its jaw, and the blow was so intense that the sword pierced the top of the dragon's mouth. He spun around the dragon and sliced its head off with his other sword. Uriel joined Israfel and other angels in a fight against many human-sized dragons.

151

Above them, Raphael flew, dodging dragons and griffins. He jabbed his halberd through the neck of an oncoming beast. The dragon shot a cone of ice at the angel and froze one of his wings. The two plummeted toward the surface. The dragon whipped its tail at Raphael's throat and pulled him closer to its claws. Raphael twisted his halberd in the dragon's neck and drew his sword as the dragon tried to squeeze the air out of him with its tail. Uriel came to the aid of his best friend, launching arrows with lightning speed. The dragon was forced to let Raphael go. He tumbled to the ground, landing on his iced wing, which fortunately broke his fall.

Another dragon flew to Uriel's flank but was stopped by a large spear. The fire from its mouth shot a few feet above the angel's head. The spear cut through the dragon's wing and pierced its chest. Israfel was about to throw another spear but was forced to defend himself against other beasts. Before the dragon had time to react, one arrow punctured its eye, and a volley of others smacked into its body. The dragon still managed to fly, even though it was coated in its own blood, when an angel swooped past, severing its head.

Uriel rushed down to aid Raphael. He quickly folded his bow and slapped it on his back, flinging the quiver of arrows to the side. He drew his two swords from the sheaths. He defended Raphael from danger and moved with incredible speed as creatures from the Earth and dragons moved in to kill one of the Heavenly Seven.

All around the battlefield, the Fey continued to enter the nostrils and ears of dragons. They took down many more, but they suffered massive casualties. An ancient fire dragon incinerated many fey with one breath. Other dragons killed hundreds of fey with a swift whip of their tails. The fey were elusive, but the dragons were foes that were difficult to contend with.

In the darkened sky, Draaheson soared in the air, killing angels with his razor-sharp claws and his powerful jaws. He fired out a line of lightning from his mouth and a cone of magical energy with his claw, destroying many angels on the ground. As he curved up in the air, he projected a blast of fire from his mouth and set several angels on fire. They attacked him with arrows and spears, but most didn't penetrate his hide or cause any more harm than a momentary tickle. He looked to the outer edges of the battle and saw an abundant use of magic. He shifted directions and flew toward it. No one was able to challenge the unstoppable shön dragon. He slapped angels to the ground like flies that were in his way.

On the edges of the battleground, several powerful spell casters used their abilities to aid in the battle. Leading this group were Zachriel and Gabriel. They launched spells of destruction on the opposition and spells of protection upon their fellow angels. Protected by a group of lower-ranking angels, they were calm and confident. Gabriel shot numerous blasts of white energy that caused the creatures of Earth to crumble or evaporate in an instant. Zachriel tried to protect angels from spells cast against them and physical harm from the dragons. He shifted the earth to create a wall blocking acid blast. He moved a boulder, and it instantly snapped a griffin's neck in the air.

An elite guard of angels did their job of protecting the spell-casting angels and their two commanders. Some of the angels were there only to heal the wounded that were brought to them. But as the angels continued their magical assaults, Draaheson dove down and shot a massive funnel of fire from his mouth. Gabriel, Zachriel, and the others jumped out of the way but were singed by it. Gabriel and Zachriel put out any flames on their clothes and got to their feet. Both started to cast a spell of protection. Suddenly, an enormous earth elemental emerged from the ground and grabbed them before they could complete it.

Chapter 33

Azrael continued to observe, but the battle moved closer to his position. A sizable griffin noticed him in the distance and altered his course. Azrael spotted an ominous shadow behind him. He tumbled quickly to his left, and the griffin's talons scratched the ground where he had been standing. Azrael shot out his white wings and sprang into the air away from a pair of boulders. The griffin came around for another pass and pursued Azrael through the sky. It shot balls of green energy at him. He tucked his wings into his body and shot down to the ground like a blazing arrow to avoid the blasts. Azrael expanded his wings to slow down and flapped furiously to increase his speed. The griffin caught up, snapping and clawing at him.

"I am not going to fight you," Azrael stated.

The two spun in the air, but Azrael did not try to strike out. He avoided the attacks and did not retaliate, even when the griffin snapped his beak down at Azrael and caught him off guard. The angel drew his two swords to block the second strike. He shoved the griffin back and flipped in the air before the mouth could close down on him. The angered griffin shrieked and charged at him. It smashed into Azrael and forced him down to the ground. Azrael tried to break free of the griffin's claw as they fell toward a tree. Azrael's irises turned a light blue that was almost white as he pried himself loose. They crashed into the tree, and Azrael avoided the impact. However, he could not avoid the griffin clamping him again with his claw. The griffin moved in for the kill.

"Stop!" Mother Earth commanded.

An invisible wave crashed into the griffin and knocked it flat. Azrael readied his blades for another attack, but Mother Earth's command traveled across the battle and was heard by everyone. There was complete silence and no movement by either side for a moment. But then the fighting resumed.

"Leave the pupil of the Seven be," Mother Earth declared. The griffin slunk off, snarling.

Azrael sheathed his swords. He dropped to one knee and gazed into Mother Earth's fire-like eyes. "Please, let me have the soil and end this destruction and death."

"You are not going to try to take it from me?" Mother Earth asked.

Azrael paused for only a moment. He knew he was destined to complete this task; it had to be done. But he sensed this wasn't the time for violence, and perhaps that particular aspect was not meant for him.

"No, I am only going to ask you. I will return empty-handed if need be. But I refuse to fight you."

"Why?" she asked curiously.

"Because I understand why you wish to withhold this gift from us, though it is what God has commanded. Though many may suffer, in the end, I see the good that will come from this exchange, and I would not have such suffering be the catalyst."

Mother Earth could not only see how genuine Azrael's expression and words were, but she could also feel it in her being. She felt his kindness and compassion and knew this angel—and no other—was the one to whom she would give a handful of her precious Earth soil. Though it pained her, she was pleased it would be to one such as him. "I will give it to you on one condition."

"What is it?" Azrael asked.

"As time passes, I know that some of the creatures of this world will fade away. I do not wish that to happen to them. Would you take some of them to Aeirliel, to Paradise, so that they may fall under the protection of the Angelic?" she requested.

155

"I would be happy and honored to take those you hold dear and keep them safe."

"Even ones I do not hold dear?" Mother Earth asked.

He waited. "Such as?"

"The mermaids and other creatures who are not so kind."

"Of course," Azrael agreed.

She caused water to flow from the pool into her being from underground. Mixed with the water was the Earth it had gathered. She handed the pinches of soil to Azrael.

"Then, upon this agreement, Azrael, I give my most precious soil to you."

He took it and placed it in his pouch. "Thank you. But what of this battle?"

Mother Earth looked into the chaos and destruction, and her eyes were ignited with fire. "Wait here. I will end it."

She sank into the ground and surfaced in the middle of the battle. The childlike figure of Mother Earth walked amidst the butchery without the slightest worry or concern for herself. She broke apart into the four elements and disappeared. The ground began to shake and vibrate with fury. The elements of the Earth ceased their attacks. But the dragons in the air continued to fight.

"I said, that's enough," Mother Earth's voice bellowed across the battlefield.

Enormous rock arms burst out from underground and snatched several dragons and griffins. Zachriel and Gabriel were placed on the ground by colossal earth elemental that had grabbed them earlier.

What is this? Draaheson asked with fury.

The voice of Mother Earth echoed from the clouds above. "This battle is over. The soil has been given to Azrael. I shall not fight the Angelic or any other force sent by God."

156

If you do not aid us in destroying the Angelic, we will do it ourselves! Draaheson bellowed. Drool sizzled out of his mouth and off his razor-sharp teeth. He let out a long, deafening roar. Despite the warning, he lashed out at Gabriel and Zachriel. He cut both of them with his long claws. Suddenly, though, he struggled against a force. It dragged him with all his might into the ground. But that would not stop one of the most powerful dragons in creation. He broke free of the land and started to fly when a colossal fist from the Earth snatched him back.

The dragons that heeded Draaheson's roar pursued their offensive. Those who had once been their allies had now become their enemies. The elements of the Earth turned on them. The dragons quickly realized that their efforts were for nothing and halted their attacks as each of them was surrounded.

"Should you or any of your followers continue their attacks against the Angelic and the fey, I will destroy all of you," Mother Earth's voice trumpeted across the battleground.

Draaheson struggled to break free. However, the strength of Mother Earth surpassed even him. He knew that without her support, he could not win.

Very well. But we will not forget your betrayal today. He warned. *When we return to Earth, we shall be far stronger than you are now.*

The gigantic earth-made hand released Draaheson. He let out a long and loud roar for all of his companions. The surviving griffins and dragons took to the air and opened black gateways to travel back to their plane of existence in Aeirliel. Each of the elements of the Earth shifted back into their original form; the earth elementals crumbled; the fire elementals sizzled into smoke; the air elementals blew away

157

like the wind; and the water elementals were absorbed into the ground.

Among the many fallen, Uriel knelt beside Raphael. The wounds on his body were deep and near vital organs. He might have already died if not for his Angelic soul and blood. The wounds of angels healed fast, but not as fast as Lucifer's. The rest of the Heavenly Seven were older than most angels and did heal faster than them. Uriel knew he had to stop the bleeding, or no matter how quickly Raphael could regenerate, he would not survive. Raphael's wounds were already bound tightly with cloth, but it was not enough. Uriel breathed calmly as he moved his glowing hands over Raphael. Finally, he completed the rigorous task of closing the deepest wound. He sat and waited.

Raphael groaned slightly. "So, you do know how to heal after all. And here I thought I was dead," he spoke without opening his eyes.

"I've learned a trick or two from a close friend," Uriel responded.

"Oh really? Is this friend of yours extremely handsome with an incredible sense of humor?" Raphael managed to say.

Uriel sighed in relief. "He likes to think he is both. But truthfully, I think you have my friend mistaken for me."

Raphael started to laugh, but his wounds hurt, and he groaned.

****

Mother Earth reformed back on the ground, pulling elements from around her and taking her normal shape. "It is over now, Azrael."

"Thank you."

"I feel we will meet again in the distant future. Where will you go now?"

"To rescue Amy. Do you know where she is?"

Mother Earth's eyes expanded, and she saw the past events on her planet through the eyes of her creatures and the four elements. She located the day Amy had been taken and watched the event unfold. "Draaheson's people took her. She is in Aeirliel, but I do not know the exact location. I only saw the gateway to that world."

"They have most likely taken her somewhere in the southern continent." Azrael reasoned.

"I am sorry I cannot do more."

He smiled. "You have done plenty. Thank you."

Mother Earth surprised him with a hug. Azrael dropped to one knee and returned the hug.

"I wish you well, Azrael, the pupil of the Seven. If ever you need me, I am here for you. And I have one last gift to help you in your new quest."

Azrael's unicorn friend trotted out of the nearby forest, ready to be ridden.

"He is alive? How?" He asked in wonder.

"I did not allow him to die. I, too, love this unicorn, and he still needs a name. Such nobility cannot cease to exist without at least a name to remember when telling his great deeds."

Azrael moved toward the unicorn and soothingly stroked its neck. The unicorn seemed to be at complete ease with his touch. "I shall call you Sahir. What do you think?"

Sahir nickered and nuzzled Azrael with approval.

"He wants to help you. I put a spell on his horn to aid you in finding Amy. As his horn glows brighter, it means you are closer to your love."

Azrael looked from Sahir to Mother Earth. "Thank you both for everything."

Azrael mounted Sahir, waved his arm, and a blue sphere portal opened. They entered the doorway to cross back into the land of Aeirliel. They came out in the desert area of the Badlands. Dark gray clouds covered the sky. They slowly trotted in a circle, Azrael watching for a change in Sahir's horn. There was a faint glow to the east, and Azrael urged Sahir into a canter.

Chapter 34

On the once frenzied and massive battleground lay the dead and wounded. Angels mourned the deaths of their brothers and sisters, though they wasted no time starting to heal the injured. Some died just the same. The Angelic did not only heal their own; they also tended to the griffins and dragons in need. The fey also tended to their injured, with Opal Eye helping where he could.

Lucifer stood on a hill, his sword planted firmly in the ground beside him, gazing at the devastation. Seeing his brothers and sisters dead both pained and angered his heart. This battle was different from previous ones. The cause was not entirely for the Heavens. It was for a creation that had yet to prove its value or purpose. For that reason, he was angry. The loss of any angel hurt him. But for this? He was not looking forward to the creation of the mortal and felt it was not as crucial as his Father wanted him to believe. He saw nothing but dark and stormy things in the wake of the human's creation. As he thought more about this, his anger began to rise.

"I do not believe I have heard such grim thoughts from you. Not since the early Dragon Wars," Lilith said as she quietly approached.

Lucifer's anger quickly dimmed at the sound of her voice. "I did not know my thoughts were so loud. My apologies."

"No need to apologize to me, Lucifer. I can understand why you feel as you do. I have seen grim things with these mortals, as you have," Lilith assured him.

"I am unsure if I should speak to the Father or anyone about this. But after seeing this battle and what may lie ahead, I cannot think the mortal is good." Lucifer spoke his doubts and frustrations.

162

As he spoke, clouds seemed to cover the light upon his body until, for a moment, he was in a dark shadow. He saw Michael, and the shadow over him faded. "Let us go to Michael and Uriel," he suggested.

Lilith and Lucifer teleported from where they stood to a mere fifteen feet from Michael, who held a dead angel in his arms. He sighed heavily as he closed the eyelids of his fallen comrade.

Uriel put his hand on Michael's shoulder and held out his hand to help him to his feet. Uriel was almost without a scratch, aside from a small cut on his forehead and one on his chest.

Michael could not say the same. He had many cuts and bruises from the battle. They were minor and did not hinder him. "We may have won this battle, but we have lost many angels and fey." He spoke with defeat.

Lucifer touched his right shoulder. "We have lost many angels, but nowhere near what it could have been. Where is our little brother, Azrael? I am sure our gratitude for so few deaths belongs to him."

"Looking for Amy, I would guess," Beelzebub spoke as he approached, sheathing one of his blades.

Beelzebub broke through the smoke as he strolled up without any sign of a wound. Though he had taken minor cuts here and there, they were not visible to their eyes. Beside him were Opal Eye and Bien. Opal Eye appeared more fatigued than anything else. He leaned heavily on his staff as he limped closer. Bien had a few wounds and struggled to fly.

"Bien, we are in debt to you. Thank you for joining us," Michael greeted him.

"Nearly all of the fey that were able, came," the fey king replied.

Lucifer nodded. "I will make sure Raphael helps with your wounded. He will have much on his plate over the next few days."

"He should be up to the task once he fully recovers," Uriel reminded Lucifer.

"I'm sure Gabriel, Zachriel, myself, and others will be able to mend most before Raphael is on his feet again," Lilith assured them.

Bien took a deep breath to steady himself. "I hope we can look forward to an era of peace after a battle like this."

"I see no reason why there cannot be an era of peace and prosperity throughout the Heavens, Aeirliel, Earth, and the entire universe." Although Lucifer spoke positive words and showed affirmative emotion for all to hear and see, under his words and skin brewed a seed of anger and pessimism that now sought water to grow.

Chapter 35

Azrael rode Sahir across the desert of the Badlands. They pushed up and down hills as the sun faded behind them. Sahir's horn dimmed as they continued, and Azrael decided to stop and dismount. He led Sahir around in small circles to see which direction they needed to take. He watched the horn carefully and finally saw it brighten. Sahir anxiously galloped off in that direction. Azrael ran after the unicorn. He shot out his white-feathered wings and flew after his brave friend.

As they reached the top of another hill, Azrael saw Crown Mountain. It was named this because it looked like a crown. Long ago, one of the first-born dragons fell from the sky and crashed upon a massive mountain. The destruction was so devasting that part of the mountain fell into the ocean, and the rest remained as a crown. It was said the head of the firstborn dragon was laid within the remaining mountain. A castle-like wall of mountains facing an ocean had five distinct points. The peaks on the mountain appeared firm and thick and had been carved to form an impenetrable fortress. A peak shaped like a castle tower was at the center of the five-mountain point formation. It was less jagged than the other four mountain peaks. It shot hundreds of yards above the rest of the mountains and rose so high that clouds and mist partially hid the summit.

A storm crept over the night, and dark gray clouds hid the moonlight as the mist slowly rained from the sky. Azrael dismounted and examined the mountainside. He noticed a small opening in the mountain that was at least a hundred yards up from the ground. He did not see any clear way to reach it on foot.

"Thank you again, Sahir. I hope I can return these many favors to you. But from here on, I must venture alone," Azrael stroked the unicorn's neck. "Do you wish to stay here or return home?"

Shair wanted to stay with his friend and was ready to battle with Azrael until the end. Azrael looked into his friend's eyes and spoke to him. *This is something I must finish on my own.* A portal opened, but it was not from Azrael but from Mother Earth. After some hesitation, the unicorn entered the portal, and it closed behind him.

Azrael flew up to the cave opening and entered it. A stream of water, which came from the ocean on the other side of the castle-like structure, flowed out from the cave. It parted to the left and right outside of the entry. Azrael swiftly moved through the dark and damp cave. His feet barely touched the ground or made a sound. He whispered the words of a spell and became invisible. He knew dragons could sense the magic of the spell, but he did not know what other dangers might dwell within this mountain. The cave was large enough to fit even the most massive of dragons. Water dripped from the walls, filling the air with the smell of the ocean. While the cave was close to total darkness, Azrael's Angelic eyes could still see, and he moved forward without worry. He pulled out one of his swords as he went. He advanced higher and higher within the mountain until he came to a central cave area with high ceilings and space beyond what mortal eyes could see.

Azrael saw Amy lying curled up on a rock surrounded by darkness. He saw a path along the outer edges of the area, though nothing connected to where Amy rested. He used another spell that levitated him off the ground, allowing him to gravitate to her silently.

She lifted her tired head from the arm it was buried in, staring into the void without a shimmer of hope in her brown tear-filled eyes. Azrael had not come for her, and she feared the worst had happened to him. A silent flash of light burst in front of her, and she jolted up. "Do not be afraid. I am here for you," murmured Azrael.

Amy's heart leaped within her body. She knew that voice. Such hope could come only from Azrael. The hope that had diminished from her eyes was restored in an instant. Azrael phased into sight and sheathed his sword.

"Azrael! I have been worried about you," she exclaimed.

"Do not worry. I am going to get you out of here. But there is a ward around you."

"The dragon said it is to prevent others from passing through. I can walk through it, but…."

"You still have not awakened your wings." Azrael easily reasoned.

"I tried," Amy said with mild defeat. "I am sorry. It hurts too much."

"It is all right. I am here now," Azrael assured her. "Walk through, and we will be on our way."

"Where is the dragon who was guarding me?" Amy asked, looking around with a worried expression.

"I do not know. He may have gone with the others to battle, but I did not see him as I entered. Come quickly, in case he may be coming back."

She walked through the ward into his arms and smiled. Azrael held on to her as they floated to the path on the outer wall. They quietly landed, and Amy hugged and kissed his cheek. She breathed a sigh of relief as she opened her eyes and let go of him but stopped and gripped his shirt. "Azrael, behind you!"

Azrael turned and thrashed out his sword. The colossal dragon clutched the wall with his razor-sharp claws. To mortal eyes, all that could be seen of Gronoch, the ancient fire dragon, was his burning bright eyes. His body was shrouded in the darkness within the mountain. But Azrael's angelic eyes could see him very well, and his ears could hear his movement along the inner walls. Unlike other creatures, dragons had ways of masking the sounds of their movements. Azrael saw that this was no ordinary dragon. He would have to be careful in every move he made.

A touching reunion. It is a shame she will have to witness your death. Gronoch greeted them with a slight growl at the end.

"The battle is over. Mother Earth gave me the soil. There is no need to fight," Azrael explained.

Because Mother Earth forfeited her soil to you, that does not mean Draaheson has given up, Gronoch replied.

"You seem familiar, dragon. May I ask your name?"

I am Gronoch. Is my name familiar? He chuckled.

Azrael had indeed heard of Gronoch. The ancient fire dragon was well known throughout the Heavens. Some of his friends had fallen to Gronoch. He had earned his reputation as one of creation's more vicious and ruthless dragons. It was rumored that he alone decimated the sixth legion, although nothing had been confirmed.

"I have heard the name Gronoch, and I know how powerful you are. If you want the soil, I will not give it to you."

Foolish angel! Gronoch bellowed as smoke sizzled out of his nose, and drool simmered on his teeth like oil burning in a pan. *I do not care if the battle is over. I do not want the soil. I also know who you are, Azrael, the pupil of the Seven. Your death would be worth boasting to every clan of the dragon empire. That is all I want.*

"I have no quarrel with you. I only came for Amy. I plan on leaving without further delay."

Gronoch smacked his tail in front of them and crushed the back of the wall behind them. Small stones fell; Azrael grabbed Amy, leaping and spinning to avoid them. Given the strength and power of this dragon, he knew using a portal would be unwise. He would not risk either of their lives for a quick escape. If a rock or some other object hit Amy or Azrael upon entering the portal, they could be lost forever from the universe's existence. The slightest disruption to the gateway or them while they enter the gateway could cause a disaster of that level.

Neither of you shall be leaving here alive!

Gronoch launched a breath of blue fire at them. Only some of the more powerful ancient fire dragons and ancient shön dragons could produce a fire that hot. With Amy in one arm and his sword in the other, Azrael sprang off the wall with one foot in the air to avoid the blast. His wings shot out, and he flew far from the dragon.

"You will be safer here," he promised Amy, setting her down in the curve of the rock wall.

Azrael immediately sprang into the air to return to his dragon opponent. He dove down with his sword pointed at Gronoch, but veered to his left to escape the dragon's snarling bite. Azrael bent smoothly and quickly, avoiding the strike to curl around for another attack. This time he fired a blast of blue energy from his free hand and smacked Gronoch in the head to prevent him from taking flight. The explosion took Gronoch off guard, and he fell backward into the wall. He quickly recovered and whipped his tail at Azrael. The angel flattened and curled his wings against his back as he flew under Gronoch's tail, his face barely avoiding the blow.

Gronoch leaped back on the wall and shot small fire energy bursts from his eyes. Azrael flew as fast as he could to avoid the fire behind him. The bursts hit the cave wall, and rocks tumbled down from the blasts. Azrael was hit on the back by a rock and fell to the ground. He quickly extended his sword against the wall to slow his fall. He recovered and flipped in the air, nimble as a gymnast, to land on his feet. *This angel is a worthy adversary,* Gronoch observed to himself. He would take great pride in killing Azrael. He knew that Azrael was highly praised amongst the ranks of the angels. It was clear to Gronoch that he would have to adjust his tactics to gain the upper hand. He needed Azrael to lose his composure and focus. It was the fastest way to get through his defenses. At that moment, he knew the hole in this angel's armor. He glared at Azrael, and his eyes glowed red with fury.

Azrael studied the dragon as it slowly crept along the wall. He would not underestimate this dragon and could only hope that he could stall it long enough for help to come. He did not believe he could defeat it.

Gronoch ended the stand-off between the two by leaping off the wall with his wings flapping and flying swiftly at Amy. Azrael moved to intercept him, but he knew he could not fly quickly enough. Gronoch slowed his speed as he came within feet of Amy. She backed up against the wall and crouched down. The dragon dug his claws into the wall as he landed above Amy, upside down.

Amy threw a rock at the dragon's eye. Gronoch growled and belched fire, but as soon as he did, Azrael appeared out of thin air and jammed his sword into the neck of the beast. Gronoch's head twisted as the flame poured out of his mouth. Amy narrowly avoided the fire.

Azrael knew he could not beat the dragon to Amy through the speed of flight but could get to her faster by teleporting as Beelzebub had taught him. He had to be careful to use his magic sparingly. Teleporting was not an easy spell, and he did not want to use up his magic too soon. This would be a long, hard fight.

The dragon bellowed and smacked Azrael into the wall with his claw. Gronoch grabbed the angel and smashed him into the wall again, bringing his mouth down to chop at Azrael. But Azrael swung his sword up through the bottom of the dragon's colossal jaw and forced Gronoch's face into the wall on his left side. He roared in pain and loosened his grip enough for Azrael to escape. While Gronoch's goal was to make Azrael lose focus, he lost sight of his intended prey, and in his anger, he pursued Azrael instead of Amy.

Gronoch was furious. He wanted nothing more than to slay the puny angel. The two combatants soared around the cave area, with Azrael able to easily maneuver his more athletic body. Gronoch did not have that luxury. His body and wingspan were so huge that he had to be careful not to hit pillars as they flew. Azrael tucked and curled around the pillars, making it difficult for Gronoch to catch him. Fireballs shot past the angel and crashed into the cave walls. After circling through the cave, Azrael feinted as if he were going to ascend before dropping below and under Gronoch. Before the bulky dragon had time to react, he collided with the wall. The cave wall crashed open to the night, revealing clouds pouring rain.

Gronoch wrapped his tail around Azrael's waist and pulled him outside into the murky downpour. Azrael cut off the end of the dragon's tail with his sword. Gronoch shot more blue fire from his mouth, lighting the rain-filled night. Azrael avoided most of the flame, and the rain helped cool the minor burns he received. Meanwhile, he shot blasts of bright white energy at numerous places on the dragon. Gronoch could avoid a few white energy projectiles, but others hit him, causing severe burns that bled.

The blue flames and white energy blasts could be seen miles away under the sinister rain. For Amy, the sight was easy to see from only a few hundred yards. She could do nothing but watch helplessly from the cave opening. The duel pushed forward, and she hoped that her love could defeat the dragon.

Gronoch got close to Azrael, clawing and biting at him rapidly. Azrael blocked and avoided the attacks as best as he could under the heavy rain. He tried to stab Gronoch's claw but was hit with the other claw across the side. He maneuvered away from the dragon with blood dripping from numerous injuries. He saw Amy standing at the cave opening and took a deep breath. He knew what he had to do, no matter the cost.

Azrael moved with astonishing speed around the dragon and wounded it in countless places. Gronoch blew a massive breath of fire, and it cindered one of the angel's wings. Azrael dive bombed at the dragon and spun to his right as he avoided a ferocious bite. He grasped the top of Gronoch's wing and punctured it with his sword. He let gravity pull him down and drew his other sword to block attacks from the dragon. Azrael withdrew his sword from the dragon's wing and took another brutal scrape from Gronoch. But the angel persisted and used both his blades to cut off the remaining portion of the dragon's wing. Now, neither of the two could fly.

The pupil of the Heavenly Seven grabbed the dragon's tail and used it to spring himself up Gronoch's battle-torn body. Gronoch launched lines of fire at Azrael and swiped at him with his claws. Azrael took cuts and burns from Gronoch while he stabbed his sword in the dragon's chest and dragged it as they spiraled down to the ground. Gronoch roared and attempted to dislodge him, but Azrael lept from the dragon's body to the clouds. Azrael called upon a vast amount of his magical energy to summon a spell of ice to destroy the dragon. Gronoch shot an enormous cone of fire at the angel, which missed. As the last fire breath escaped Gronoch, Azrael unleashed a ray of ice into the dragon's mouth. It froze down the dragon's throat and expanded to freeze its entire neck and head. Gronoch's body turned as Azrael ceased his blast and crashed headfirst into the surface. Gronoch's head and neck shattered into pieces, and rain poured down on his lifeless body. Azrael tried to use his one good wing to slow his fall. He managed to skid across the ground moments behind the giant dragon he had slain. He lay on the ground in exhaustion, pain sparking all over his body.

Amy felt the impact of Gronoch's landing just after she heard the mighty crash. She peered down the cliff to look for Azrael. As he was a few miles from her, she saw he was wounded but was unsure how severely. Amy searched for an easy way down to him.

Azrael slowly turned over, and the pain of his wounds surfaced. If a mortal had taken those wounds, they would already be dead. Only his Angelic blood and the remaining *maeraz* in his body kept his heart beating. However, his injuries being as profound as they were, it was amazing even for an angel to still be alive. Azrael suffered six cracked ribs and deep gashes in his sides and along his left leg. One of his lungs had been punctured, and his heart had been grazed by one of the dragon's claws. He had lost most of his blood, and his complexion was pale. Most Seraphim would be barely able to move, but not him. He would not quit or give up. The one thing keeping him going was Amy. He rose to his feet, each movement more painful than the last.

Azrael turned his azure eyes up the towering mountainside and saw Amy's long, flowing hair blowing in the wind. A smile crossed his face. Somehow, he found the strength to limp forward and flap his wings. He lifted twenty feet in the air, even though one of his wings could barely

174

move. But he could not get any higher; the pain was too great. He fell next to the mountainside and grasped the wall. His body shook as he pulled himself up the mountainside. This was who Azrael was. If he could not fly, he would walk. If he could not walk, he would crawl. No matter what he must do, he will never give up. Azrael lost his grip, fell, and pounded into the ground, bruising his shoulder. Neither his will nor his heart would quit, but his body slowly drifted away.

Amy saw Azrael's efforts and knew she must get to him. She tried once again to force her wings out. She could feel her wings stretch the skin and muscles in her back. It felt like a baby trying to rip its way through her back. The pain was too much for her. She fell to her knees as the rain dripped on her body. She fought back the tears and helplessness. Azrael had saved her countless times; now he needed her, and she was crippled by pain.

No! she thought to herself.

She would not let her fears get the best of her. She rose to her feet and went back inside the mountain. Amy took a long deep breath and sprinted out of the cracked mountainside. She leaped off the edge and began to fall. She closed her eyes tightly and clutched her fists as she spun in the air. Her black wings shot from her back, covered in crimson blood, as a shaft of moonlight glistened through the dark rain clouds. She flapped her wings, though it caused an aching pain, and she had no experience in flying. She descended to the ground while gritting her teeth against the soreness as her blood was washed away from the rain. She fought the wind as she flew for the first time. She crashed on the ground, gashing her knees, twisting her ankle, and scraping her elbows raw.

Amy's wet black hair draped over her face as she rose, muddied from the rain. She lifted herself from the ground, covered in mud, blood, and bruises. She limped over to

Azrael, who lay very still. She knelt and enveloped him in her arms while wrapping her blood-covered wings around him. The two lay together, each covered in their set of wounds. The rain lightened to a mist, and the moonlight illuminated the couple as though it were a spotlight. Amy hugged and kissed Azrael's cheek. Her hands shook, and her lips quivered as tears flowed down her cheeks. The only way to tell she was crying was from her expression as the rain streamed down her face.

Azrael's breath became fainter and fainter. His heartbeat, which normally pounded like a drum, now sounded like the highest key on a piano.

"Azrael, I'm here. Please don't leave me. I'll stay right here with you. I do not know what else I can do," she held him tighter with her wings and tried to will any strength she had left into him.

Azrael was drifting in and out of consciousness. Somehow, he heard her words like a distant echo traveling through a cave of darkness. He saw a dim light from where the voice came and was drawn to it. For a moment, he regained consciousness and managed to speak.

"Do not be…afraid. I am…here for…you," he faintly spoke as he put his hand on hers and squeezed it firmly.

The words he had said countless times made her cry even harder, and she held him closer. But as he finished speaking, his grip on her hand loosened, and it seemed they would be the last words she would ever hear from him. Once again, they were together, and once again, they would be separated. But this time, it would be permanent.

At that moment, Amy realized the extraordinary. "I am not afraid for me. Because of you, I am not afraid for myself. Only you, my love, am I afraid for." She knew the certainty would fade, but just now, as he fought for her and now lay broken beside her, it was true.

"Please, Azrael, you're strong. I know you are. Please do not leave me. I love you."

Suddenly, Amy felt an invisible wave pass through her being. It was the presence of another being. She was unsure who or what as a shadow covered her and Azrael. Her vision was slightly blurred because of the amount of blood she had lost from flying after her wings were awakened. An angel would usually never attempt to fly right after their wings had awakened because of the danger. She slowly turned her head to see who it was. She could not distinguish the face of the being that quickly came to their aid.

"Do not worry. I will help him," the voice assured her.

She recognized the voice and smiled. The panic in her heart quieted, though she was still worried about Azrael. The mysterious figure worked furiously on Azrael. It was clear the being was experienced in healing, as it knew what had to be done first. Azrael had lost a lot of blood, but his heart needed to pump once again. There was a bright blue glow, followed by a white flash. Slowly Azrael's heart wound mended enough for blood to pump throughout his body. His heartbeat returned, though it was extremely faint. The figure also noticed that Amy was in need too. After a few moments and a wave of a hand, a portal shot up. Both Azrael and Amy were carefully lifted telekinetically by the mystical figure.

****

When she awoke sometime later, Amy looked around and realized she and Azrael were placed next to one another on separate beds. Amy could see lights in the room despite her vision being blurred. She heard other beings enter the room and could listen to them all talking but did not know what they were speaking of. Eventually, she passed out again. She was alive, and she trusted the angels in the room to aid her. While Amy slipped in and out of consciousness, Azrael continued his fight to live.

At his side were Gabriel, Opal Eye, and Zachriel, all very experienced healers fighting to get the blood out of his lungs and fully mend his heart. They were well-versed in Heavenly magic and the best available to tend to Azrael. The wounds were difficult to close, and multiple deep cuts were across his chest. Within Azrael's darkened and quiet mind, a small match had been struck, and a faint light continued to grow. As the wounds in his legs were closed, Lucifer joined the healers in the room. While Lucifer was not known for his healing prowess, he could still help the others progress and move on to the other wounds. Lucifer could not stay away; Azrael was his little brother, and he would do everything he could to ensure his survival. The faint match lit in Azrael's mind was slowly growing.

Chapter 36

The room was packed with scrolls and books, and weapons were mounted on the wall. The grey walls, with their black trim and the dangerous armaments, gave the room a gothic tone. It would be evident to any who knew him that it was Beelzebub's room. Azrael lay on Beelzebub's bed. His wounds had been dressed, though minor bumps and scratches were visible. His eyes were closed, and Amy sat at his side, holding his hand. She was also wearing a few white bandages around her arms. Surrounding the bed were Lucifer, Michael, and Opal Eye. Azrael slowly opened his blurred eyes.

"You gave us quite a scare, little brother," Lucifer said.

"Amy?" Azrael murmured in a low tone.

"Yes, I'm here."

They smiled at each other. Azrael's eyes regained focus. The first being he saw was the only one he had eyes for, his beautiful Amy. She looked as stunning as always. Her genuine smile was as soft as her touch.

"You should never have fought one of the ancient dragons by yourself. You're lucky to be alive," Opal Eye scolded.

"He managed." Lucifer winked at Azrael.

"I thought you had left me," Amy said softly.

"I would never leave you. Who was it that came to our aid?" He knew full well that he would not be here if someone had not rescued the two of them.

Michael grinned. "Guess."

Azrael peered around the room at everyone present. Each shook his head. He finally recognized the room and located Beelzebub leaning against the wall by the doorway of the room with his arms crossed. He smirked slyly. Azrael should have known from the moment he thought of the question: his closest and most loyal friend. Every time he had a great need or the situation was dire. Beelzebub was there for him.

Beelzebub strolled over with his confident and elegant stride.

"We will leave you three alone for a few moments. Good to have you among the living," Michael said. He, Lucifer, and Opal Eye left the room.

"How did you know where to find us?" Azrael asked.

"I have my methods. I promised you I would try to find Amy. I went to the one source that would be of assistance. She was most helpful," Beelzebub explained.

"You spoke with Verinity," Azrael surmised.

"I did. She was more familiar with the various places her kin would hide. She informed me as soon as she knew Amy's whereabouts. You found her just before I could tell you where she was."

"Thank you, Beelzebub, for everything."

"What are friends for?" he shrugged.

"I believe you still have one small task to finish." Beelzebub gestured to Azrael's pouch that held the soil.

"I do," Azrael agreed.

Chapter 37

After a few days of recovery for all the angels, the Angelic finally put to rest some different matters. The first was the end of what many hoped would be the last Dragon War. The seven ancient shön dragons had been selected by the Queen and would finally enter the gates of the Heavens.

Beelzebub stood ready to greet the dragons at the main gate of the Seventh Heaven. The gate had been rebuilt several times over the course of its existence. The wall was now hundreds of feet tall and half as thick. It was made of thick stone that looked like ivory or marble and was harder than diamonds. It stretched out for miles from the center of the gate. While the gate was not made of the same substance and appeared to be the weakest point, it was the strongest. It was reinforced with many spells and enchantments that were invisible to normal eyes. Virtually all of the Cherubim had a hand in forming the spells. The gate was made of a metallic substance that looked like gold but was a sturdier metal with a unique ability to absorb incantations.

On top of the wall were many guardian angels with bows or spears. In a time of war, there was a far greater number than today. The seven dragons approached the gate where Beelzebub stood with six other angels, ready to allow them passage.

Rnisen, the dragon spared by Lucifer in battle, was a giant ancient shön dragon with obsidian scales and a trim and fit body. He was not the biggest of the seven dragons, but he was powerful and highly regarded. The other six ancient shön dragons were Zixusamosiel, Cepiel, Dasol, Uronah, Sanetiel, and Ssaadilon—the only female dragon among the group.

"The queen apologizes for the behavior of some of her subjects and hopes that this will not cause another war between us," Rnisen declared.

"I assure you it will not," Beelzebub reassured him.

We are the seven Queen Verinity selected to join you in the Heavens. We swear to be loyal to you and the Queen. Each of us shall act as a companion to a member of the Seven.

"Then I would like to elect you to be my companion, Rnisen," Beelzebub offered.

Would you? Rnisen was surprised.

"Of course."

I am familiar with you, Beelzebub, and would be honored. I am sorry we could not help you in the recent battle. Verinity felt it best for us not to be involved. She thought we would be targets in the battle, stirring an even more significant divide amongst the dragons.

"I think she was right," Beezelbub assured him. "Do not worry; neither will we hold anything against you or the Queen. Please extend my thanks to her again for finding Amy and Azrael."

"I shall."

Beelzebub extended his arm in welcome and encouraged them through the gates.

"Welcome to the Heavens."

****

God's throne was filled with light, but did not hurt the eyes or burn the skin. The light gave a good and pure feeling to all who were present. The stairs to the throne were white and made of a soft, smooth marble stone used throughout the

183

Heavens. God stood at the top of the stairs with a magnificent smile. Before Him was a sea of angels that had no visible end.

Azrael walked up the stairs to God. He stopped and knelt as he held out his pouch. "The soil, as You asked, Father."

"Please stand up, Azrael."

Azrael stood before God, who put His hands on the angel's shoulders. God's radiant smile was more eloquent than thousands of words.

"The Mother of the Earth had only one request. She wished some of the creatures be brought to Aeirliel to dwell so they could be under Angelic protection," Azrael reported.

"It shall be done. You did better than I could have hoped. I am very pleased."

God took the pouch and emptied it into His hand. "Behold, my Angelic children, the human called Adam."

He dropped the soil from His hand, and a white glow spun within and around it. It slowly began to form the shape of a human. Then the light burst brightly and quickly faded. Adam's naked body was toned with evenly trimmed light brown hair. He blinked uncomprehendingly at the angels.

"Very good," God concluded.

The angels observed Adam, and he did the same. There was a pause as the angels, and Adam looked at one another. Neither seemed to know what to do.

There must be a way to show the human a sign of respect and make him feel at ease, Michael pondered.

It then struck him. *Brothers,* he told them, *join me in showing a sign of respect to the mortal. We should show this mortal there is nothing to fear.*

Michael stepped out amongst the crowd of angels and bowed to the human. Azrael followed his lead, and the rest of the angels knelt almost in unison. However, one angel remained on his feet with his arms crossed. One angel did not drop to his knee. That angel was Lucifer. A hint of anger and disgust crossed his face. God felt the anger among the angels and looked at Lucifer with concern. Lucifer turned away and disappeared instantly.

"Rise, My children. The humans will be creatures you protect and serve, as they do not have the abilities that the rest of you do. They shall live in Aeirliel, and you shall be their guardians in that paradise as you are for all living things."

The angels stood as one. God transported Adam to his new home and dismissed the angels to their tasks. As they scattered, chattering about the momentous day, Azrael approached God. "Father, I have a question about my relationship with Amy."

"Go on."

"We wish to be together always. We want our souls to be bonded or connected. We want Your blessing over the event."

"And so it shall be done," God assured him. "When the time comes." He winked and disappeared.

Michael came up behind Azrael and put his hand on his little brother's shoulder.

"We shall make a grand celebration for the occasion."

"What happened to Lucifer? I could feel his anger," Azrael wondered, worried about his brother.

"I am not sure," Michael said.

"Do you think he will come to our celebration?'

"I do not know. I have never felt him this angry."

Michael knew his elder brother better than anyone; their friendship had surpassed many millenniums. They had seen the worst of things and the greatest of things. Their bond was one of the strongest shared between two angels. What worried Michael most was not the anger but whether or not it would linger.

Chapter 38

Lucifer angrily paced in his room with his head down. The room was a study with contrasts, both light and dark elements. His hand brushed against the rack of long swords on the wall. He angrily knocked over a side table, sending books and scrolls crashing to the floor.

He could not believe what had transpired. A being with no proper understanding of the magics or the ways of the universe had been praised by all the angels. Even worse was Michael being the first to kneel before them. His closest friend and brother—whom he thought would see things as he saw them—were not of the same thought process. He was unsure what would come of these mortals or how he would feel about them in the future, but for now, he was not pleased. He did not know if there was anyone he could trust with his feelings.

"You can confide in me, Lucifer," Lilith spoke as she phased into sight.

Lucifer was displeased. "How did you sneak in here?"

"I have my ways."

"I do not have time, nor do I wish to speak with you now," he told her.

"You did not bow to the human," she pointed out.

Lucifer stopped pacing and looked Lilith directly in the eyes.

"Why should I bow to him or any other mortal? He has done nothing to earn our reverence or respect. He is nothing compared to any of the Angelic."

"It is true: the mortal does not have any of our strengths. But no one possesses the power you do. You are the first and the strongest of all angels. What will you do now?" Lilith asked.

"What can I do?" Lucifer asked.

Lucifer sighed and stretched out his wings, rubbing his hands along his cheeks. He was trying to figure out what to make of the whole situation. It displeased him. However, things were not as they appeared. He wondered if perhaps he was being too quick to judge.

"First, I am going to wait and see if anything changes. If not, I will take the necessary action," he decided. "Why did you come here?"

Lilith gracefully walked into the room and slid her fingertips across a chair table, ensuring he knew she saw the overturned table.

"I was curious about you. I could feel your anger and pain and wanted to let you know...." She stopped in front of him and smiled.

"Let me know what?" Lucifer's eyes narrowed.

"That I agree with you, and I am sure others loyal to you will agree."

Lucifer returned her smile with a wicked grin as the light from the candles dimmed in the room from Lucifer's power.

****

On the outer gates of the palace of the Heavenly Seven, on the stairs that lead to the entrance, Azrael stood with Beelzebub at his side, followed by Michael, Gabriel, Raphael, Uriel, Zachriel, Jrindren, and Opal Eye. A group of angels observed, dressed in ceremonial togas clasped by golden brooches and tied at the waist by fine silken belts.

Azrael and Amy beamed into one another's eyes, oblivious of everyone else. Amy's hair was laced with white ribbons and small white flowers. She wore a white gown, and Azrael wore white robes to complement her. They put a chain around each other's necks, Amy's was made of gold, and

Azrael's was made of platinum. They exchanged rings as well. Amy's ring was gold with diamonds surrounding an opal to form a rose. The engraved words in angelic writing were inside the band: "I am here for you." Azrael's ring was platinum, and inside it read: "Do not be afraid." They held hands and faced God.

God smiled at them. "Amy and Azrael, I will do something special for you." He held one hand over Azrael's heart and placed His other hand over Amy's. A white glow came from God's palms. He removed His hands, reversing their positions. As He once more touched their hearts, the white light disappeared.

"You are now the first ever Angelic soulmates. I wish you eternal love and happiness," God announced.

They would be forever linked to one another. They would be able to feel each other in ways others could not. God would show this unique ability to the angels to allow for more unions.

Azrael and Amy kissed and pulled away, smiling at each other. All of the angels cheered and clapped. Beelzebub grasped Azrael's shoulder. Six of the Seven congratulated the couple, proud of their pupil. Peace and happiness swelled throughout the Heavens and the universe. Azrael was overjoyed to have this union with Amy and pleased to see so many in attendance, supporting them, but there was one thing missing. There was a void to his right where Lucifer should have stood.

"Where is Lucifer?" he asked, but no one could answer his question.

There was little else that could be done to make this day better. Azrael was not sure if he should be concerned about Lucifer or not. He did not understand Lucifer's reaction and hoped his anger toward the humans would change over time.

Unable to stay away altogether, Lucifer watched from a distance. He felt separated from the ceremony and his brothers and sisters. He could not share in their happiness and peace. From this separation, a great divide would occur unlike anything ever seen. But that is another tale…

Made in the USA
Middletown, DE
28 October 2023

41434154R00123